Elroy Bode's

SKETCHBOOK II

Portraits in Nostalgia

Introduction by

EVAN HAYWOOD ANTONE

Drawings by

FRANK O'LEARY

TEXAS WESTERN PRESS

THE UNIVERSITY OF TEXAS AT EL PASO

Library of Congress Catalog Card No. 70-170986

ISBN NO. 0-87404-032-9

Typographic Arrangement by

CARL HERTZOG

INTRODUCTION

By EVAN HAYWOOD ANTONE

THIS VOLUME *needs no introduction to the thousands of readers who first met Elroy Bode in his* Texas Sketchbook, *issued by Texas Western Press in 1967, or to those who have read his work in various regional and national publications such as* Southwest Review *and* Redbook.

For those who have not yet experienced the spell of enchantment which Elroy Bode can weave, perhaps an introductory word will be of value.

For over a century, writers have been trying to capture creatively the special flavor of the land and the people of Texas. Many have succeeded in capturing a section or a part. For example, William Humphrey captures East Texas in Home from the Hills *and* The Ordways; *Larry McMurtry conveys the loneliness of the Texas plains country in* The Last Picture Show; *Paul Horgan writes symbolically of Texas in* Whitewater; *Tom Lea transfers the vastness of the El Paso Southwest into* The Wonderful Country; *Edna Ferber's* Giant *portrays the world of oil-rich Texas ranchers. All of these writers have realized what George Sessions Perry stated in his* Texas A World in Itself — *Texas is so large geographically that so divergent ethnically, that it refuses to be captured by a single artist in a single work.*

Over a hundred years ago, a poet named Walt Whitman tried to capture his United States and to put that nation into Leaves of Grass. *In his* Preface *to the 1855 edition, Whitman reached the conclusion that "the United States themselves are essentially the greatest poem" and that a great poet is one who can record* every experience of that land with simplicity — "the sunshine of the light of letters is simplicity." Hopefully, such a writer would be absorbed as affectionately by his land "as he has absorbed it."

Obviously the precepts advocated by Whitman have guided Bode in his creative efforts, for he has embraced all of Texas and absorbed it. He was born and raised in the Texas heartland and this is his first love. But he also loves Galveston and the Gulf coast; he sketches with fidelity the people of East Texas; he captures with accuracy the Plains country and the Panhandle region. His second home is West Texas and the border cities of Juarez, Mexico and El Paso, Texas where he now lives, teaches, and writes.

Hopefully, he will continue to write about his Texas, either in sketches or perhaps in longer works — novellas or novels. Whatever his choice, he will write in prose which reads at times like poetry, which sings at moments and breathes life into the land and the people. This is the thing he does so well. This is the reason his Sketchbook II will enhance his reputation as one of the most truthful of Texas writers in the 1970s.

J. Frank Dobie maintained that he never wrote about his own section of the country "merely as a patriotic duty." Instead, he wrote and taught about the Southwest "because I love it, because it interests me, talks to me, appeals to my imagination, warms my emotions." For those same reasons, Dobie believed that others who live in the Southwest "will lead fuller and richer lives if they become aware of what it holds." Elroy Bode agrees, and through his writing does as much as one man can to promote this awareness.

CONTENTS

Crider's 1

A Day at Palo Alto 6

   I   Teddy Mudge 6
  II   White Butterflies 7
  III   Eight Boys 9
  IV   The Director 9
  V   Mountain Top 11
  VI   Mark Jacobson 13
  VII   The River 14
  VIII   Dusk 17

Texas Journal 20

  I   As a Nurse 20
  II   The Henry's 21
  III   Nut 25
  IV   Sanctuary 28
  V   Rip 29
  VI   At the Ewell House 30
  VII   Cafe 31
  VIII   Across from Honey's Bar-B-Q . . 32

Billings Feed and Hardware . . . 37

Heartland 49

  I   Rabbit, at Sundown 49
  II   San Antonio Streets in Summertime 50
  III   Old Maid 51
  IV   Ranch Woman on the Phone . . . 52
  V   Sally-from-the-country 53
  VI   Pilot 55
  VII   St. Anne of Dallas Mutual . . . 55
  VIII   Johnnie 57
  IX   Young Bride 59
  X   Clark 61
  XI   Initiation at Mesa Verde 62

Home 64

  I   Summer (Ages 3-8) 64
  II   Fall (Ages 9-11) 67
  III   Winter (Ages 12-14) 71
  IV   Spring (Ages 15-17) 74

A Case of Survival 80

CONTENTS

Texas Journal 86
    I   Clearing the Air 86
   II Betty Lee 87
  III Beer 88
  IV Sunday Women 88
   V Lucia 90
  VI Knowing 92
 VII A Small, Mild Man 93
VIII In San Elizario 93

In the Bus Station 97
   I   Shoeshine 97
  II The Slowly Walking Fellow . . . 98
  III No Scales in Pomona 99
  IV Off to Vietnam 101
   V A Man 102
  VI Ab Snopes 104
 VII Not Many Flars on the Grave . . 106

At the Border 109
   I   Contentment, and Milky Ways . . 109
  II Crying Man 110
  III Jodl, of the Blighted Area . . . 112
  IV Maids from Juarez 116
   V Negro on the Bench 117
  VI Bathroom Joys 119
 VII The Scotsman 121
VIII Woman at the Bar 122
  IX Pan 124
   X Juarez — Summer Days 125
  XI Eric the Red 126

Texas Journal 128
   I   Counter Girl 128
  II Fields, Mountains, Clouds . . . 128
  III Robin Hood 129
  IV Solitary Women 131
   V Tom 131
  VI Grona's Lumber Yard 133
 VII They Should Have Been There . . 136

Portraits in Nostalgia 139

A Saturday Visitor 145

Suzy 148

Zzzz The Clown 155

Elroy Bode's SKETCHBOOK II

Crider's

W PROBABLY no one in the hill country — certainly not old man Crider — thought you could take a slab of cement, add some benches and a wire fence, and end up with a gold mine. Yet he did exactly that. And it turned out to be the best kind of gold mine, actually, not dependent on limited veins of ore but on unlimited human beings — on the twenty-five cents they will pay for a can of beer and the dollar bill admission they will dig up for Saturday night. So far, there is no indication that people or their money will ever play out, and Crider's seems destined to remain as solvent as any hill country bank.

There seem to be at least two Crider's — the one you go to, say, on a Saturday night and the one you might see the following day. A tourist, going for a Sunday drive along the river road west of Kerrville and suddenly coming upon Crider's at three o'clock in the afternoon, will most probably pull his Oldsmobile off the pavement and ask his wife, incredulously, "You mean this is where we went to last night?" For daytime Crider's, minus the acres of parked cars, the blaring music, the sight and sense of people dancing and drinking and milling around, is wholly un-prepossessing. Its essentials stand out sharply in all their bare country homeliness: the empty field of smooth cement, the small covered bandstand down at one end, the green tables and benches and big drooping oaks leading at the opposite end into the two room cafe-kitchen. In the glare of a hot three o'clock Crider's looks quite deserted and forlorn — the kind of place to buy a coke in maybe or a package of cigarettes and then move on past.

But as the day softens — as the sun fades behind the cedar-covered hills and the nearby river greenery darkens into a long, lush stage backdrop — Crider's gradually reveals its virtues like a brilliant night flower starting to bloom. It becomes a fine place to rest from the day's labors. You can get yourself a cold can of beer from the cafe and come outside under the oak trees and sit down at one of the tables, and everything — the hill country, the river, the coming to an end of another summer afternoon—seems very right and pleasant. And if it happens to be a Saturday you can look out past the dance-floor and see that already a couple of cars with horse trailers are parked down at the large, bleachered corral, unloading for the Crider's rodeo.

It's entirely pleasing at dusk — but just let night fall and the whole visual world lie dead and buried beneath the central Texas blackness. Let eight o'clock, eight-thirty, nine o'clock come. Let the summer camp bugles finally sound taps up and down the river and the off-duty counselors start for their cars; and the tourists from Houston and Dallas and Port Arthur begin to get bored with the quietness of their summer lodges; and high school kids from Kerrville get tired of driving back and forth along the same familiar streets; and the cedar choppers from Hunt and Ingram start rattling down country roads toward the main highways and home. Let darkness cover the land and people begin to feel the need for a place of light, a place to gather and drink a beer or two or more, a place to be private within yourself if you want it or be unrestrainedly lively but nevertheless a place to be in the midst of others. Let these conditions exist and Crider's becomes a thing beyond the sum of its benches, trees, and strings of colored lights. It becomes The Good Place Up The River, the yellow-bulbed oasis in a vast black desert of night.

SATURDAY NIGHT is always the big night, of course. There is a string band — sometimes a local, inexperienced group from Kerrville or Fredericksburg, usually a more professional outfit from Austin or San Antonio — and extra counters set up for beer and cold drinks and the customary dollar admission charge. There are always several members of the Crider family working at the gate — one collecting the dollar bills in a cigar box and the other stamping a black circular receipt on the back of each customer's hand: "Crider's, Since 1925."

Crider's has no specialized clientele. Indeed, the whole charm of it lies in the unselfconscious mingling of people who would ordinarily never rub shoulders except in a movie script — rustic and sophisticate, oil man and grounds keeper, college drama instructor and high school majorette. Where else would an aging Houston dowager hold tightly to the muscular arm of a young six-foot-six horse wrangler from a summer girls' camp as they make their way to the dance floor to try a German *schottische?* Where could the son of a Leakey truck driver order a Bireley's orange for the daughter of a Dallas banker? Where would the female lead of "Finian's Rainbow" — the summer stock "Finian" showing nightly downriver at the Arts Foundation — slap her delectable thigh in such unrestrained laughter at the tales of a Rocksprings bachelor who raises Poland China hogs? Where, also, could a balding little man climb on a table-top and do a prolonged, Yogi-like headstand to the cheers and handclappings of the on-lookers — or chin himself half a dozen times from an overhanging limb — and then, his nightly ritual over, grab the arm of some pretty woman forty years his junior and go strutting off to the dance floor to put-his-little-foot?

The peak time of Saturday night is from ten o'clock until one. The rodeo at the corral is generally over by ten, and the crowd and performers from it begin to drift in along with late-comers who first went to a show in town or a private party. Since the few tables under the oaks are always taken early, the overflow has to distribute itself about in little standing groups or on the narrow wooden benches scattered along the fence. The phalanx of young stags that rather loosely blocks one end of the dance floor early in the evening begins to edge solidly forward — like a school of curious fish intent on observing more closely a band of deep sea divers. And in the anonymity of the flowing, shifting crowd a highly reserved doctor from Kerrville may find himself throwing aloofness to the winds and dancing a very loose-legged polka with his eleven-year-old daughter; or a hard-swallowing young camp counselor may finally approach the table of a tanned, beautiful woman twice his age — the mother of one of his "boys" — and ask her to dance and have her smile up at him with a very definite and pleased yes. It never seems to matter particularly who does what; it's just accepted that you come to Crider's to let your hair down.

But even if most people come to Crider's to be in the big middle of things — the dancing, the jostling back and forth to reach tables or the beer counter, the laughing, the flirting — there are some who are content just to remain outside and watch. They sit on the fenders of their cars, holding babies, smoking, chewing on matches. Primarily they are family folks who can't afford a dollar for themselves and their kids so they come early and park along the fence and look. Now and then a few of the men will saunter down the line of cars to the outside beer counter and hunker outside the rim of bright lights. They exchange handshakes — the single, brief little respectful jerk of country and ranch people — and then join in with the gazing toward the noise and music and lights. Perhaps before long a barefooted boy will slide out of the darkness and stand next to his father — not saying anything at first, just watching and listening to the quiet steady talk of the men, then finally speaking down to his father: Mama wants you. The man nods and reaches a slow arm around the boy's legs. He says, All right, run along; I'll be there in a minute — and after a while he rises and nods toward the group and moves on back toward his car.

As THE HOURS slip on by toward one o'clock and the cars begin to circle out of the big dusty parking area, one of the hill country's unsolved puzzles reoccurs. By all logic, the high-geared, drink-laden drivers of so many fast-moving cars along such a narrow, twisting, up-and-down river road should provide accident headlines each Sunday morning. Yet despite curves, beer, and one-arm-around-the-girl driving, the road in from Crider's has remained incredibly accident-free. It's as though some kind of special, pilot-light shrewdness remains lit even in the most bleary-eyed of drivers, saying, "Look, just keep your wits about you and you can make it — you got to be up here again next week, you know." And like a flock of tipsy homing pigeons they all go racing back through the darkness into town.

A Day at Palo Alto

1 : *Teddy Mudge*

W HE DID NOT want to come so high. While the other boys yelled and dug wildly into the side of the cliff for fossils, Teddy Mudge sat in jumbled leaves under a wild cherry tree and sniffled. Yellow-haired, blue-eyed, his pale legs scratched from the hard climbing, he looked down at the dirtied laces of his new tennis shoes and gave another little sudden sniff of crying. His canteen had spilled on his new Palo Alto T-shirt and the pocket of his short pants had ripped on a persimmon limb. And he had dust in his nose. He sniffed and looked between his legs at the leaves: he did not see the point of climbing a mountain if your legs got skinned and dirt got in your eyes and nose — especially if you hated climbing anyway.

He touched his newly scraped knee where it was sticky, and wanted very badly to go back down into camp. He wanted to go into his cool cabin and blow soap bubbles through his hands in the bathroom, or listen to his tennis shoes as he flopped around in them across the cabin floor. He wanted to scratch a nail file across one of the rusty window screens and watch the dust puff away outside. He wanted to go to the tennis court and run after tennis balls for a counselor — and then get tired and bored and go around to the back door of the dining hall to see if Jennie Mae had any cookies.

Teddy Mudge looked down through the tree tops to the camp grounds and wished he were there. He wished he did not take nature study. He wished his knee were not skinned and his shorts weren't torn.

Then, as he was wishing, he saw a spider's web shining in a crooked cedar tree. At the center a big green spider with a hump on its back was coming out of its spider hole with slow, watchful steps. For a while the spider simply clung there to its gently rocking web—casually, contentedly, like an acrobat riding a safety net after dropping from a trapeze bar. Then something happened: maybe there was a shift in the morning breeze, or a cedar branch swaying across the sunlight. Maybe it was just some mysterious and instinctive skittishness aroused inside the spider itself. Anyway, whatever the cause, it was enough, and just as the big green spider with the hump on its back was beginning to rock most gracefully in its web, it suddenly turned tail and ran. It lunged backward into its hole like a flustered old woman throwing up her hands and fleeing from the sound of a squeaking mouse. And Teddy Mudge, watching the spider disappear, rubbed his arm across his nose and threw back his head — and giggled, through dangling tears. ⋑

II : *White Butterflies*

🦋 THE TEN O'CLOCK SKY was a hard blue and the sun was burning down through a magnifying glass of clear shining air as the nature counselor led his class into the walnut flat along the river. Here small walnut trees grew thickly and a long stretch of clean, sun-bleached rocks lay in the old dry-branch fork of the river bed.

The counselor stopped and sat down on a cypress stump and let the boys explore for a while. A killdeer soon ran crying across the rocks and the boys started after it, making shrill piping sounds like the killdeer and laughing. There was brown debris from the last flood still lodged in the top branches of the walnuts, and as the boys passed by they stopped and raised their hands above their heads toward the matted sticks and leaves — marveling that they were actually standing on the spot where a flood once was. They quickly forgot the killdeer and began turning over big rocks to see what was underneath. As they looked they found a mother scorpion with many small amber children huddled on her back, and one small cool-black snake, and occasionally trap-door spiders who rushed out of their holes to see what was the matter.

It did not take long for the boys to become lost from time and from themselves. They strung out along the flat, poking and prying and feeling rough things with their hands. The blood went to their heads from so much bending, and with the close heady smells coming from the walnut blooms and the damp river bank and the hot sun on the rocks, they soon became a little drunk. Whenever they would finish exploring under a tree they would start off suddenly in brief half-dazed runs, hearing nothing but the sound of the smooth rocks crunching together beneath their shoes, seeing only the bright glare of the sun.

It was in such a condition—their mouths open from unformed, excited thoughts and sweat circling neatly beneath their eyes — that they suddenly saw jerk into view out of the trees a pair of white butterflies. Perhaps it was simply the heat of the morning and the dizziness of too much running about along the old river bed, but as the butterflies danced together above their hands in elaborate and tantalizing wildness the boys saw right through the wings and their delicate motion into forgotten dreams and imaginings — into pictures of clipper ships, smoke trails, dancing elves. They watched, fascinated, and then before their eyes the fragile wisps of their dreams scattered off in a little white zigzag trail above the jungle of walnuts, disappearing like bits of morning vapor into the wide blueness of the sky.

III : *Eight Boys*

ⓦ IT IS AFTER LUNCH and eight boys lie on cots in their cabin, reading funny books. Although they suck thumbs and dig idly into their noses and now and then pinch or pull at their tight bathing suits, they never take their eyes from their reading. They lie passive and content, dressed for the free swim period that will come when rest hour is over.

Eight boys, resting — very lean and satiny-brown now in mid-July but not obvious in their growth, not even having definite rear ends yet. They are still developing with the clean, embryonic lines of childhood. Their bodies do not shout strength and hairiness as they will later; calves and biceps are not yet bunched in muscularity. There is no awkward excess. Every line is still the simple straight line of a boy.

Eight boys, with only their little washboard chests rising and falling to give testimony of the tireless motors inside. They are soon to yawn and stretch and let the funny books slide from their cots to the floor. Then, just as effortlessly, they themselves will slide into two o'clock drowsiness, the silence of the cabin continuing to float on their slow and even breaths.

Eight boys, nine years old, more attuned to the pulse of a warm afternoon than they ever will be again — for they are still part of it. Some unseen placenta of the day still gives them nourishment, preparing them for that disconcerting moment in the future when they will be born, wild-eyed and awkward, into adolescence. **ᴈ**

IV : *The Director*

ⓦ DURING THE REST HOUR, just before the counselors' afternoon bridge game starts in the office, the camp director makes his brief after-dinner rounds: he readjusts water sprinklers under the big pecan trees by the infirmary, he bends indulgently to pick up stray gum wrappers by the dining hall, he gets a ping pong ball out of a lantana bush next to the aquarium, he finds a wet sock in the grass beside the tennis court. He walks along, bending and straightening and retrieving — and does not mind at all. He likes being the caretaker of summertime souls and bodies. He likes anticipating and dealing with all the little failures of the flesh. He is a contented man, a middle-aged catcher in the rye.

He walks along at two o'clock with his jaunty canvas-shoe gait, springing a bit on his toes, never hurrying yet never idling. As he makes his way behind the long row of cabins he hears the whispered warnings of the campers: "Shhh, here comes Hal, y'all!" He moves past each cabin blandly, never indicating that he hears the smothered giggles and the bare running feet. He passes on by and enters the big community latrine (will he find the towels in the commode: — Cabin 7 holds its breath); after a few moments he comes out the other side, the heavy latrine door swinging shut behind him with a sound so familiar and anticipated that had any other sound followed the director's exit entire cabins of watching and listening and even sleeping boys would have sat up simultaneously in their beds, transfixed by wonder and awe.

The director continues his tour beneath the big shady Spanish oak trees until he reaches the last cabin, Cabin 12. He stands beside it a moment, looking about — at the baseball field lying across the fence in the glaring sun, at the long stretch of greenery down at the river — then turns and starts his walk back. If the director had been a more passionate or impulsive man, it is possible that as he smelled the hot grass and pungent cedar posts and blooming flowers which were all around him he would have voiced a sighing, prayerful oath. He would have given way to his sense of great peace — his delight at how nice it was to walk in the two o'clock summertime beauty of Palo Alto. But the director said nothing. Instead he just smiled somewhere deep inside himself, picked up another gum wrapper from the ground, and walked on in his jaunty, relaxed way toward the office and the counselor bridge game.　　　　　　　　　　　　　🙠

v : *Mountain Top*

🌿 ONLY AN HOUR AGO the smiling-eyed riding instructor had shifted his buttocks on the patio chair — skillfully, as though they were instruments he had mastered — and generously using his friendly smile, with its many obedient wrinkles, he had assured the mother that the camp horses were good ones and gentle and that Luanne would be perfectly safe. And the mother on her cool summerhouse patio had jangled the white bracelets on her slim brown arms and poured more ice in her glass and sat smiling: she was obviously pleased. She had watched through the patio screen as the two of them rode across the low-water bridge back into Camp Palo Alto and on up the mountain trail: he, suntanned and authentically western-looking, with an orange plastic lanyard hung around his neck and his muscular legs sausage-tight in his jeans; and her girl, slim and blonde, with caliche dust from the road already beginning to powder her expensive riding boots.

And now they were riding along the mountain ridge above camp. Below them, in the white cabins, it was still rest hour. The camp area, from above, was mainly a thick covering of oak and cedar trees, but they could catch a glimpse of flag and a few white patches of the tennis court and gravel drives. They stilled their horses at the rim and the riding instructor pointed out across the bare grounds of the baseball fields to the long line of cypress trees that meant the river. Sighting along his outstretched arm, the girl searched out her summer home among the many similar squares of rambling lawns. As he gradually lowered his arm she saw the riding stables north of camp and the horses looking small and toy-like there. "We'll try to get back down before rest period's over," he said. He looked at his watch. "But we still have time to go see the rifle range." He took off his big-brimmed Stetson and dragged his sweating forearm across the red hat-line on his brow, then replaced the Stetson firmly at exactly its old slant. He grinned his broad, friendly grin and slapped Luanne's knee and said to his horse, "Let's go, Jiggs!"

They turned away from the ridge and headed straight across the top of the mountain. To reach the rifle range they would have to turn right and go down into a long shaded hollow. But they didn't make it to the rifle range. A little way down the trail the riding instructor reined up, dismounted, and tied both horses loosely to the branch of a cedar tree. He helped his girl get down and kissed her a long time as they stood there beside the horses — and then he took her to the ground. Without words being passed, the brown riding instructor asked and the mother's blonde daughter said yes and the two of them were down in the leaves and hot needle grass, in a whole mountain top of quiet, in a whole afternoon of pulsing July fever.

(As the minutes passed grasshoppers flew out of the grass, sailed along in a fierce brittle snapping, then dropped back into the grass again, as though felled suddenly by the great heat

(Long thin leaves of mesquite trees hung in a plumb-straight greenness, like socks on a line or many bats sleeping: hanging as if trying to remain cool through sheer inactivity

(Lizards waited on the tops of big flint mounds — suspicious, watchful, their necks frozen to one side: looking as if they had stopped in all the stillness and heat to catch a faint hollow voice from deep inside the earth, perhaps one of God's left over from eons past

(Purple wine cups wobbled along the trail as little breezes touched them, and out in the clearings small yellow daisies shook almost all the time, making a yellow shimmer in the bright afternoon air

(Unseen insects on the mountain top kept up their steady drone; occasionally a dove would call in its lonely detached way out of some distant hollow

(And it was not long before the horses, straining forward a little after grass, pulled their reins free from the branch of the cedar tree and began eating their way, unhurriedly, back toward the ridge.)

Sometime during the afternoon one of the camp cooks gave four quick strokes on the dining hall gong, signaling the end of rest hour. On the mountain top a cricket heard the sounds coming faintly across the ridge, and he quickly gave one single short answer from his home under a rock. Grazing along through the alternate patches of shade and brightness among the Spanish oak trees, the two riderless horses raised their heads once as if they might have heard the sounds too, but went on chewing. Farther back on the mountain top, stretched side by side in the leaves and shade, the riding instructor and his girl heard the sounds. They listened a moment, then somehow found gongs as good a reason as any to smile at one another again and touch each other's hands and kiss. ⮞

VI : *Mark Jacobson*

❧ HE WAS BACK against the cabin wall, facing the others with his head lowered and his shoulder thrust protectively toward his chin: Mark Jacobson, age nine, a Jewish boy with *petit mal* and a nose like a shovelbilled shark. He was in trouble again, and his large handsome eyes were full of tears.

They were ringed in front of him, a fierce little jury in wet bathing suits. They crowded him, giving repeated shoulder shoves that left wet spots on his white T-shirt and orange shorts. Mark had broken a model airplane while the others were at free swim, and now the owner of the plane was sitting forlornly on his steamer trunk with the model balanced awkwardly in the palm of his hand — surrounded by loyal defenders but almost crying too.

Mark rubbed his nose against his shoulder, leaving a smear of mucus, and the jury stopped their pushing and began to point and laugh. He slid along the wall and lifted his shoulder a little higher. He wanted to do something to make them stop, but all he could think to do was put his hands over his ears and yell: "Shut up, shut up, shut up!" — and then try to glare at them fiercely from behind his tears.

Finally Mark gave in. The jury was jumping up and down, pointing at the smear on his shirt, when he pulled his mouth down into a raw-red half moon, closed his eyes, and began to cry. A little bag of mucus was blowing in and out of his nostril as they began to hit him.   ⋑

VII : *The River*

🌱 THE CAMP TENNIS instructor had himself a favorite place down at the river. It was where the sycamores grew thick among the cypress trees and the river was shallow and clear over a sandy bottom. The bank was shady in the afternoon, and small perch were always waiting around near the edge without ever seeming to move — as if painted in the water. The tennis instructor like to come down after his last class to sit with his back against one of the big cypress trees and smell the clean river freshness and hear coming downstream the sound of water rushing across a layer of rocks. It was a pleasant, secluded spot — a place to read in and have private thoughts.

One afternoon he laid his book aside and decided he would do something he had not done a half dozen times in his life: he would get into the water. He would pull off his watch and T-shirt and tennis shoes and while there was no one around to see, he would carefully step into the water and walk around on the sandy bottom.

He couldn't really say why he did not know how to swim. As a boy he had been sick a good deal and had not learned then. But he could have tried to learn later if he had really cared to. It was just a thing he had neglected — and now, at thirty-five, he was too ashamed to admit that he didn't know how.

He took off his tennis shoes and put his watch and T-shirt beside them. He already had on his swimming suit from tennis class. The sun was down low, cutting through the trees with slashes of yellow light like huge guillotine blades, and as the tennis instructor stepped into the water he noticed how deeply the sunlight penetrated it and how the small perch did not run from him but just backed away, curious and unafraid. The water was warm and as it gradually rose up his calves and above his knees, the tennis instructor began to feel a deep pleasure in it — almost a completely new kind of rapport with it and the world and life. The sand was easy to walk on, giving away with each step just enough to make it seem that he was floating along or walking in slow motion. He gave himself little shudders of nervous delight at the thrill of actually being there in the water under so many tall trees and during such a warm, golden time of day.

When he got to the middle of the stream the surface was still only up to his thighs. He purposefully splashed himself and rubbed his chest and arms, trying to work up an even more intimate feeling toward the water. As the chillbumps spread over his body from the sudden coolness and from his excitement, he thought: Now if I will only keep this up every day for a week or two — until I become completely at ease in water and won't be the least bit reluctant or apprehensive — then I'll come right out with it and tell Hal I can't swim but that I want to learn. He could teach me privately during rest hour. Damn it, it's something I should have done a long time ago. . . .

The tennis instructor began walking slowly up the middle of the river toward the bend where he heard the water rushing peacefully over the layer of rocks. He knew he ought to be getting back — it was getting close to supper time and the boys would almost be finished with their showers. But he was enjoying the water too much and the smells of the trees and ferns and the feeling of the warm, filtering touch of the sun: he would wade on a little farther and then get out and run all the way back to camp, drying off along the way in the late-afternoon breeze.

So he quickly began to splash his way forward — and stepped past a ledge into a five-foot hole and drowned. He could have easily saved himself. All he had to do was recover his balance and stand up. He was over six feet tall. But he fought at the water, trying to stay afloat, and his feet never touched the sand any more. He choked and swallowed water and could never get his breath long enough. Two other counselors found him late that night — still in the water hole, surrounded by a ring of small perch that seemed to be staring back into the yellow glare of the flashlights, not moving, highly curious, unafraid.

VIII : *Dusk*

❦ AFTER SUPPER WAS OVER the athletic young Negro cooks moved about in the deserted dining hall like human-shaped, gas-filled black balloons. They floated through their clean-up chores without any effort or hurry, swinging cuptowels loosely in the air at nothing, humming, feinting at each other in passing with an elbow or knee and then doubling over across a table with silent wild laughter — making the hall seem for a while as if it housed a lazy, shadowed carousel. Within the hour, though, they finished with their work, changed into their town clothes, and were rattling down the back service road in the camp pick-up, their laughter seeming to fade gradually behind them out of the cab into the twilight itself.

In the dining hall kitchen Hattie Mae, the white dietician, and Moses, the aged yard man, lingered over their after-work cups of coffee. Hattie Mae sat in a cane-bottomed rocking chair, smoking some, idly tapping her long moccasined feet to a vague inner rhythm. Occasionally, if she happened to smell the honeysuckle vines outside the kitchen door or heard a few distant peaceful voices coming from some far-off part of camp, she would hum a little from a Baptist hymn. Moses was usually content just to sip at the cold coffee and smoke his pipe and generate incredible body odors.

During the summer months night was always a long time in coming after supper. Twilight seemed to hold the land in the grip of an endless pause before finally relaxing and allowing it to slip quickly into darkness. And in this long interim, when all sounds seemed to be coming from places that were farther away than usual and when the smells of the river and the trees clung more familiarly to the air, the boys of Palo Alto wandered about the great grassy areas of camp until it was time for call to cabins. Sometimes there would be tribe competition — baseball, capture the flag, tennis matches — and the last reserves of energy would be neatly drained away. But on free nights, with supper filling their stomachs and with life's unknown excitements perhaps still lurking somewhere, the boys roamed about in a dogged, restless way — exploring. Sometimes they went to the nature study hut on the side of the hill and looked at the snakes sleeping in their shadowed cages and at the tarantulas that crawled mechanically around in bottles on limber furry legs. Sometimes they hid from one another in closed-off, secret places where they did not dare to move: where they sat cooped up for what seemed like hours with the strangely foreign sound of their own hearts beating as pursuers searched closer and closer. Sometimes, at the deepest part of the twilight, the air would be filled by hundreds of amiably blinking lightning bugs, drifting along underneath the trees like herds of miniature glowing cattle that were grazing their way to new pasturelands. The boys would get jars from their cabins and run after them wildly across the yards — catching a few and watching them pulse their yellow lights as they crawled slowly against the glass.

Suddenly, when no one was expecting it and yet when everyone was finally ready for it, the camp loudspeaker would come on. The needle would slip onto the old worn grooves of the call-to-quarters record, a moment or two would pass with just the familiar scratching, and then there would be the friendly, wavering, rather lonesome sound of the bugle. It always managed to say, in the calm, sober way that the river or the mountains around camp might say it: "All right, now, the day is finally over and night is here. We're all tired so let's put everything away and get ready for bed. We'll pick up our routines again tomorrow."

When the last note of the bugle faded away everyone knew it would be fifteen minutes until lights out. Counselors began walking in the darkness toward their cabins — stopping along the way to allow small campers to hitch a ride on their backs.

Doors opened and slammed down the long line of cabins, and there were last-minute toilet flushings and shrill talking and periodic warnings from the counselors on duty: "O.K., just a few more minutes . . . let's get everything done — Leslie, get those funny books off the floor." Then as the record of taps came over the speaker, the lights would go out one by one in the cabins and for the rest of the night the only sounds in camp were katydids calling back and forth in the trees and the breathing of many small bodies stilled peacefully in sleep.

Texas Journal

1 : *As a Nurse*

W EVEN THOUGH she had not put on the white uniform when I knew her, Victoria looked, acted, even thought like a nurse. Since that time as a child when she held her sister's bleeding foot in a coffee can full of kerosene and then wrapped it up with her brother's yellow scout handkerchief, Victoria was destined for service — geared for the dedication of her brisk, breezy smile and strong limbs to those she could help when they were in pain.

She had the clean brown hair a nurse should have in order to be truly nurse-like: hair that always looked as if it had been washed and put up in curlers and brushed out with familiar strokes just before breakfast, then given a few touches of her hand and dismissed at the mirror with a critical accepting look. Too, she had the mild swinging gait of someone used to covering endless corridors: used to walking briefly into many rooms and then briskly out again. The walk was not poise-conscious; neither was it primed with sex. It merely showed that regardless of the professional duties she happened to have, she was a female first of all, a female with hips that lived. (Even in quiet, sobered wards you could visualize them moving like halves of a gently waving sign that read: A Woman, Not Just Competence, Inhabits This Skirt).

She also smiled like a nurse, but here too the woman smiled first and the-nurse-within merely agreed. Her smiles came with a genuine ease — with the same ease that breathing comes, as if she simply liked the good natural feeling that spreading her mouth always gave her. The smiles would remain on her face a while, like guests who knew they were welcomed to call and made themselves at home.

Victoria was the kind of young woman that doctors first come to rely on professionally and then, in a gradual way, emotionally. She had a clear and obvious intelligence that could be utilized quickly, in its full bulk. It was a definite, circumscribed thing there in her head that functioned efficiently — the way a hand does — and she or anyone else was welcomed to its use. And most importantly, it was free and uncommitted, not — as is the case so often with a man's brain — allied with any dark, tentacled regions buried within itself. In short, it operated like the good, complicated machine the brain is supposed to be.

Victoria did not desire to know more than what was necessary for her happiness. She understood instinctively the things she needed to learn — understood without even feeling a need to hunt for them. Thus she was always free simply to be herself: to settle down in the midst of humanity and begin to serve.   ⋑

II : *The Henry's*

👥 FROM MY ROOM below I could hear their nightly murmurings in the upstairs bedroom and the periodic creak of old carpeted boards as Sammy Joe padded slowly and heavily about in his house shoes. Each night as I studied I listened to their sounds and visualized them up there: little birdlike Mrs. Henry, perched in bed underneath her reading lamp, her hair up in curlers and covered by a faded cotton cap, looking like the small wizened white goddess of some jungle tribe reading to her big faithful eunuch: a little old lady with a little old lady's weak, quavering, ceaseless voice that was actually less of a voice than a vocal leash that led Sammy Joe around. And Sammy Joe, the large, soft, nearly handsome man turning distinguished-gray: I could hear his loose, flopping loafers crossing and re-crossing the bedroom floor and occasionally his quick, explosive laugh — *huh-huhht!* — that was always faintly echoed by Mrs. Henry's gleaming little *hee-hee-hee.* I heard the raising of windows on warm nights in spring and their heavy shutting on chilly nights in fall — and occasionally the sound of a typewriter — but otherwise the nights were always the same: the heavy padding about of Sammy Joe and the small, filtered voice of Mrs. Henry.

Both mother and son were early risers. Mrs. Henry was usually outside in the back yard by six or six-thirty, pulling feebly at grass in her flower beds or standing under the tall pecan trees and trying to knock down pecans with a broom. Sammy Joe would be in the front room rocking chair by the east window, stroking the big house cat in his lap and reading the morning paper. His heavy legs would be crossed, with one loafer dangling and moving like a pendulum as he read and mechanically swung his foot. If Mrs. Henry happened to come back inside the house — to get a coffee can for her dab of pecans or maybe some kind of gardening tool from the screened-in back porch — Sammy Joe would call out to her some item he had just read in the paper: "Mama, guess what . . . Agnes Crosswhite was in a car wreck yesterday afternoon and broke both her legs." Then he would quickly whip the paper shut, draw his head back to a listening pose, and wait for Mrs. Henry to answer with her little "Whoooo-ooo" from the porch — a weak cry which meant anything from "You Don't Say" to "My Lands!" to "I Told You So." After hearing Mrs. Henry register her comment, Sammy Joe would unfold the paper again, adjust it for a little better light from the window, and continue his reading. Boots, the cat, slept blissfully on.

A good deal of Sammy Joe's morning each day was spent on the telephone. It began ringing early and he would pad out of the living room into the dark hallway, lift up the receiver and say *hullo* — with a kind of unemotional directness that made it a one-syllable word. If the caller was a telephone solicitor or had the wrong number Sammy Joe would say a short "Yes" or "No" or "We-don't-want-any-goodbye" — or "This-is-five-six-nine-two-seven" — and each response would be delivered the same way, with the same lack of interest or courtesy. His words simply entered the receiver in the flat and unconcerned way that his loafers slapped the floor.

However, if the caller was one of Sammy Joe's middle-aged women friends who rang up daily to gossip, he would say, "Oh, hullo, Verna," and collapse into the nearby wicker chair — one big soft leg draped across the other, his free arm laid across his rising and falling stomach like a piece of spongy driftwood. Usually these conversations — to Verna, the branch librarian, or Grace, the bedridden hypochondriac — lasted for thirty minutes or more, and as Sammy Joe remained settled back in his chair it was as though he were perfectly content to spend eternity there in a kind of Homeric indolence. Occasionally, as the talk became more animated, he would direct one of his *huh-huhht* bursts of laughter toward the ceiling, and Mrs. Henry would peek into the hall from a doorway to see if Sammy Joe was going to share some little anecdote with her.

Except for the small back porch and the front sitting room the house was kept in a perpetual semidarkness, with Sammy Joe and Mrs. Henry — and on rare occasions Boots, the cat — moving about inside like different-sized fish swimming through very deep waters. Actually, it is debatable whether Boots moved at all. When he was not curled up in Sammy Joe's lap in the living room he was lying on the top of the kitchen table — old and fat, a huge amorphous lump. Sometimes at night I would go into the kitchen to get ice water from the refrigerator and there he would be: The Gray Presence, watching. Raising just the barest possible tip of his tail and holding his eyes squarely upon me, he would patiently wait me out as I opened the refrigerator and poured the ice water from the vinegar jar into a glass. Only after I had shut the refrigerator door and turned toward the light switch would he start lowering his tail and closing his eyes — satisfied, finally, that the intruder was leaving his domain.

Supposedly, Sammy Joe was staying at home "to take care of Mama." But that was just for the record, of course. Everyone in the neighborhood knew it was the other way around — that Mrs. Henry, though well along in her eighties, needed very little in the way of moral or physical support; that it was Sammy Joe who was being sustained within the shadowed old rooms of the Henry house. He had suffered asthma as a boy — still had it every now and then, Mrs. Henry told me — and that was one of the reasons why he had to remain there in El Paso. They had tried Dallas and San Antonio and Houston while Mr. Henry was alive, she said, but the humidity was just too much for Sammy Joe; they always had to come back to dry El Paso in order for him to breathe. Mrs. Henry took special pains to tell how Sammy Joe wrote poetry and gave book reviews sometimes, so it was not as though he wasn't *working*.

Their needs were very simple and except for an occasional Sunday morning outing to church Mrs. Henry never left the house. Sammy Joe went out only to buy the groceries. Each morning at exactly eleven-thirty he would put on his dark glasses and go into the kitchen to ask Mrs. Henry what she needed from the Safeway store down the street. Sometimes I would be in my room, studying, and I would hear the back gate drag against the cement walk — Sammy Joe never left by the front door, always the back — and out my window I could see him move from the shade of the tall pecan trees along the fence into the naked brightness of the sidewalk. As he took his first, deceptively casual look around the street and then stepped off in his waddling, somewhat femininely determined way, the question never failed to rise in my mind: What, exactly, were the dark glasses for, and what would he do without them? Was he wearing them merely to see better against the bright sun, as anyone might suppose, or did he put them on in order to face the world? I always wondered what would have happened if a person had suddenly yanked off the glasses and said, "I see you, Sammy Joe!" Somehow I had the feeling that he might have begun to melt there on the sidewalk — until finally nothing would have been left but the glasses and the bundle of empty clothes.   ⋟

III : *Nut*

W SHE WAS DRESSED the way eccentric old Apple Annies usually are: tennis shoes without socks; a long shabby coat full of tatters and holes; a worn scarf that did very little to control the dry wisps of hair that strung out above her forehead.

I watched her in the downtown El Paso plaza as she walked about and wrote in a small blue spiral notebook. Standing perfectly still and cradling the notebook in one hand, she would write for ten minutes at a stretch; then after walking a short way she would stop — the heel of one tennis shoe arrested in midstep — and bending her head down toward her notebook she would write some more.

Most of the bench idlers took her in stride, not paying her much attention. Perhaps they accepted her as one of themselves, only in just a little worse shape. But one grizzle-bearded ex-New Yorker with a huge paunch and a yachtsman's cap seemed bothered by her: "Look at dat nut," he would say to whoever was seated beside him. "She oughtta be locked up, runnin off like dat at da mout. It just don't sound good, somebody talkin like dat in da pahk." And he would frown, shaking his head and big belly, and then breathe a little harder with his asthma.

I was in the park only once when she started on a talking spree, and her pacing was as curious as her monologue: it was as though she was declaiming inside a zoo cage, moving back and forth in a constrained and tireless prowl. She never acknowledged the presence of a passerby, and even when she would halt to specifically address an empty bench or a building across the street she never really seemed to focus on it. She just seemed to be musing violently to herself in the private world of her little blue notebook and her hates.

It was not quite clear what her total complaint was — she stopped too often in the middle of one tirade to begin another — but primarily she was down on Mrs. Roosevelt and the Catholics. She paced along, first talking to her tennis shoes or the pigeons on the grass about "Catholic abominations," then sliding right on into "old Eleanor Roosevelt" and the New Deal. At one point she enumerated a long list of peoples of the world — Ethiopians,

Senegalese, Chileans, Koreans, Vietnamese — and though I did not get the connection between the list and Eleanor Roosevelt I was surprised at how knowledgeably she rattled off the names. She spoke in a rich, throaty, drawling voice that would have been rather pleasant to listen to if she had not been using it as vent for such venom and hate. She had a crooked front tooth and a kind Humphrey Bogart slant to her jaw when she spoke, and they helped to give her words an added spit and snarl.

She was extremely tanned from years of walking about outdoors, and from a distance her face seemed rather vague — nondescript brown parts sewed together with wrinkles. She resembled, as much as anything, some kind of mad monk whose face is always kept hidden within the shadow of his dark cowl. Yet when I finally saw her face up close, and clearly, it was not that of an old woman at all.

She had paused right next to my bench, not to write in her notebook but just to stare off into her special corridor of space. I looked up, and instead of her face being truly old, it seemed more like a movie starlet's that had been made up rather poorly to resemble a Bowery grandmother. Somehow the wrinkles were not part of the skin but seemed superimposed — almost extraneous to it, like smudges of dirt. And despite the lines and roughening effect of years in the sun, the features were still astonishingly soft and somehow even innocent. The lips were like those of a young girl — very tender and full — and the eyes were clear and well-defined, without any wrinkles or pouches.

I was in the midst of an urge to take a cloth and wash the tan and dirt and wrinkles away — to see what she really looked like underneath — when suddenly she moved on. She reached inside her coat, scratched fiercely along her collarbone and underneath her arm, then began walking out of the plaza in her bobbing, long-gaited stride — looking down to the cracks in the sidewalk and giving Old Eleanor hell. ⧽

IV : *Sanctuary*

THAT LITTLE concrete porch at the front of a Baptist church in a small Texas town — I think about it, wondering what it really meant. At three o'clock on a July afternoon, when the sun had finally moved its fierceness toward the west and left the porch in an elegant shadow, what truth did the porch suggest that somehow made it memorable?

I try thinking of the little knots of faithful Baptist men and women who gather there every Sunday, in the hot times of the morning and in the cool of the afternoon. I can see them on that modest and smooth concrete, finding comfort not only as Baptists but as Baptists-joining-together-in-a-very-small-town. . . . I think of the young, untried boys in dress pants and white shirts (—indeed, Baptist Boys, soon to take on their special role as Baptist Men) who talk among themselves in the long Sunday twilights: who gather on their pants the white dust of summer from straggling clumps of Johnson grass beside the porch as they speak knowingly of things they do not understand.

Yet as I consider the porch — the way it was one hot weekday afternoon — I remember that the strong Baptist feeling was absent. It was just an ordinary square of shade — a porch offering relief to anyone who might be walking by and finding himself in need of a place to rest. . . . And that, I suppose, was at the root of the emotion I felt: The knowledge that such a small white wooden church, sitting so staunchly on its dusty side street in its hot West Texas town, was actually irrelevant to the town except for the esthetics of its cement porch. *Esthetics* . . . a Baptist church having as its only real claim to glory a pleasant bit of shade: having its porch become what the church itself had tried futilely to become for everyone, at all times and in all weathers, yet never succeeded in becoming: a refuge, a sanctuary. ⋛

v : *Rip*

HE STANDS on the corner by the Freeway Drug, mouthing a dead cigar and taking the Sunday morning air. He wears a hunter's cap, once red; a leather jacket, once new; a pair of gray pants, once clean. The two dark masses attached to his feet were probably once shoes. Indeed, everything about the man — clothes, body, the faded look of his red-rimmed eyes — is a reminder of how things once have been.

He is somewhere in his fifties, although I really can't tell. He has apparently given up on bathing and thus the dirt covering his skin tends to camouflage and deceive. It is as though the skin — stringy, shiny, tough — has hardened from lack of moisture rather than from years of work: as if the pores finally closed themselves up in sheer despair.

Watchful, strangely innocent, he peers closely at the well-dressed men who stop their cars briefly at the curb in order to stride into the drugstore for Sunday papers. He stares out at the traffic hurtling along on the overpass, and at other, slower cars moseying by on the quiet, neighboring streets. For half an hour or more he stands there beside the mailbox, sucking his lifeless cigar — looking like a grimy Rip Van Winkle who crawled into a vacant boxcar during the Depression and has just now come outside to stretch and spit and look around.

He exhales imaginary smoke from his burned-out cigar and keeps turning in little luxurious arcs. He seems to be saying to himself: Wellsir, so this is the way they do things in Fort Worth now. Hell of a note. . . .

vi : *At the Ewell House*

ON FALL SUNDAYS we turned off the Bandera highway and went down the rocky, winding dirt road that led through the Ewell pastures. When we came to the pens we parked the car

in the grassy shade of a big liveoak and walked down the slope
of a small bluff to the creek. We crossed it on flat rocks placed
there as a bridge and when we got to the other side we were
once again beneath the strange canopy of towering pecan trees.
Once again we were walking across fallen leaves through a great
still space of subdued light.

Mary and Forrest Ewell lived in a small, unpainted house that
sat in the perpetual shade of the many pecan trees. It was like a
private, bypassed little world down there — a gigantic cave, with

cave-horses rubbing against the wire fence of the yard, with
Forrest Ewell standing on the front porch, welcoming us with
his quiet, cave-dweller's smile.

It was as if the Ewells lived in a mountain cabin of Kentucky
or Tennessee: the rooms of the house were small and dark, and
a bucket of spring water and a dipper were always on a stool
beside the back door. There was a banjo and a guitar and a violin
hanging on the bedroom wall and in the late afternoon Mary

and the two children would get their instruments down and play hymns and country songs out on the porch. Forrest would spit tobacco juice over the railing into the flower bed and the juice would splatter near his collie dog. The dog would lift an eyelid for a moment and then go on sleeping while the violin scraped and Mary sang "The Old Rugged Cross."

The Ewell children, Billie Jean and Talbert, were my age and we played long hours down at the creek. It was narrow and grassy-banked and curved pleasantly out of one wooded pasture into another while small, light-brown frogs sat beside it on the sand. A spring came out of the ground beneath a big walnut tree and made a clear pool between its roots. Water cress and mint grew along the side of the pool and the round, clean rocks on the bottom looked as if they were right beneath the surface of the water — as if your nose would touch them when you lay down at the pool's edge to get a drink.

Standing beside the creek, my stomach full of fresh-tasting spring water, I would look up the bluff to where palomino horses were lazily switching their tails in the sun. Up there, at the lots, it was an ordinary fall afternoon; down along the creek, in the deep pecan-tree shadow, it was no definite time or place. It was like looking out from a dream, or a children's storybook — where life never moved or changed but stayed deep inside itself, content to remain within its own pleasing depths.

VII : *Cafe*

 I PULLED off the highway north of Beeville and went inside Rosa's Place for a cup of coffee. The screen door stuttered after me pleasantly — closing with little slow, diminishing rebounds — and as I sat in a booth next to a broad expanse of glass, I was astonished by the wealth of light in the cafe. Every corner and surface of the room was sharply revealed, as though half a dozen window shades had just been raised. It was natural, outside light, full of the clear-white vitality of the August morning.

Sitting there, I got the feeling that I was not really in a public place but had instead stepped into someone's clean and unpretentious kitchen. I drank my coffee slowly, watching the plump waitress behind the counter tend to her small maintenance jobs — washing a few pots and pans, setting potatoes on to boil for the noon hot-lunch. I was glad that such duties were carried on in plain view of the customer instead of being hidden in some ill-lit back room. . . . I thought of other cafes and the sullen, stubble-bearded old men in their small cook's cap and dirty apron who always come out of the kitchen like tubercular genies: who take one private, hostile look around before silently picking up their load of dirty dishes and disappearing through the swinging doors. . . . There, in Rosa's Place, the neatly aproned waitress did it all: she served the cups of coffee, rang up change at the cash register, cooked an occasional egg or hamburger, and kept returning to the pleasant-smelling soapy waters in her rectangular tub. With her back turned to the customers at the counter she would talk idly to them as she lifted glasses and cups from the tub and waved them dry.

There was still a hint of fresh paint in the cafe — a gleaming wall showed that it had been redone — and it mingled nicely with the smell of the hot sweet rolls and coffee. I drew a deep breath and wished I could stay in my booth by the window a little longer. I wanted to sip other slow cups of coffee and sample more deeply the cafe's comfortable atmosphere. But I thought of the long drive to Dallas still ahead, and sighed, and told the waitress: "Half a cup more and I guess that'll have to do it." The waitress nodded, and after wiping her shining brown arms on a cuptowel she reached for the handle of the steaming coffee urn and began to pour. 🐦

VIII : *Across from Honey's Bar-B-Q*

🐦 IT WAS A FIERCELY HOT Galveston noon. As I eased beneath the projecting roof of an old building near Post Office Street I felt a nice breeze coming around the corner so I sank down on an empty bench, glad to take a break in my morning's walk and have a long look around.

I had passed through these streets two summers before; little seemed to have changed. There was still the heavy, depressive, July heat, the worn-out wooden buildings, the gray lifeless air. The same slow, jogging rhythm of Negro jukebox tunes was coming out of nearby bars. Negro men still moved aimlessly from one corner to another. And over on Post Office, two blocks away, Negro prostitutes still sat on their porches, calling out, "Baby . . . hey, baby, look over here and see what I got."

Across the street from my bench, to the left of Honey's Bar-B-Q, a thin, sullen Negro woman sat on the front steps of a rundown house, cursing and complaining and spitting. An old woman sat beside her, taking occasional swigs from a pint of whiskey. The sullen woman was bent over, her arms deep in the lap of her dress, and every minute or two she would blurt out an obscenity before spitting contemptuously out into the sidewalk. Each time she spat and cursed the old woman fell forward to her knees, shaking for a while in violent, silent laughter.

On the other side of Honey's a group of men were gathered in front of a small drycleaning shop. They were talking and laughing quietly in the shade of the roof. One of them, a slender man with sharp, Nordic features, sat off by himself in the doorway of the cleaning shop, paying no attention to what was going on around him. He had on a worn, double-breasted suit with big lapels; a wide-brimmed, dipped-down hat of the '30s; black shoes without socks. Every now and then he took an unlit pipe from his mouth and cradled it contentedly in his hand while he smiled a wide, private, beautiful smile into the empty doorway.

It was after a crippled man in a three-wheeled cart had steered himself past my bench — had stopped, reached under a dirty blanket to take a pull from his bottle of Thunderbird wine, then steered painfully on around the corner — that I began to notice a mild-faced, middle-aged Negro woman who was sitting nearby in a parked car. She kept fanning herself briskly and apparently was waiting for her husband to return from Honey's barbeque place. With her glasses, neat appearance, and graying hair parted severely in the middle, she had the look of a conscientious Negro school teacher.

As we sat there — the woman in her hot car, looking out; I next to the building on my shaded bench — I began to speculate: What was going through the woman's mind — more precisely, what was she thinking about me, a young white man sitting in a well-known Negro redlight district? Looking out from the front seat of her car, the sun glinting off her glasses, was she merely saying to herself: "Oh, my, it depresses me, stopping here like this . . . I wish Eugene wouldn't always *take* so long . . . I can't wait to get on home to my nice street and my nice house and yard."

Was that her reaction: A middle-class statement of July discomfort? Or was she perhaps glancing at me and thinking: "Why in the world does *he* want to come around here, anyway. . . . See all this and then go away saying, 'Negroes are dirty' or 'Negroes are shiftless' or 'Negroes live like animals in old houses that are falling down.' . . . Shoot, *I* don't live in a house that is dirty and falling down. And *my* husband has himself a job — a good one. . . . If the white man wants to see Negroes, he ought to go where *decent* people live."

Or did she even bother with any of that: Was she, instead, looking out at me from her deceptively mild, school-teacherish eyes, and thinking: "He's the cause of it all, him and that white face sitting there so innocent-like in the shade. *Resting*, I suppose. . . . Well, he'll think *resting* before people finally get through with him. . . ."

The door of Honey's finally opened and a man in a brown hat and white shirt came out carrying a paper sack with grease spots showing on the sides. He did not exchange greetings with the cluster of men nearby but instead crossed directly to his car. The woman stopped her fanning, she talked briefly to the man as he started the car, then they drove away.

I watched the car until it was only a speck on the long, almost perfectly straight street that went across town toward the bay. I wondered if that was a Saturday-noon ritual with them: stopping by for some of Honey's barbeque on their way home from the business district, then moving rather quickly out of the depressing Post Office area into their nicer section of town.

As I got up from the bench and moved on out into the heat — to walk past more ramshackled houses, more slow-moving men — I wondered: Can a white person talk to Negroes now? The woman in the car, paused in a neighborhood unredeemed by any hope or beauty or grace: Did she blame me and my kind for Post Office Street? The sullen woman, with her arms thrust deep in her lap: When she spat into the sidewalk was she spitting at me, or life, or fate, or herself — or all together?

What *was* hidden in these faces, and would it ever be possible to know before it was too late — before knowing, finally, did not matter? ⇒

Billings Feed and Hardware

❧ IT'S A MONDAY MORNING at ten o'clock and I can visualize my father seated at the feed store behind his big dusty rolltop desk, examining the weekly ravages of his athlete's foot. He has his right shoe and sock off — very old-fashioned, high-top black shoe, very old black silk sock — and he is gingerly handling his toes so that the broken skin shows up more clearly in the light of the dangling overhead bulb. Without looking he reaches for his yellow can of Dr. Scholl's on the desk, and gingerly pours and works in the powder between the toes.

My father does not hurry with his treatment, since this is no longer the kind of moment that is stolen out of the day's rush. Now some years back it used to be that on Monday mornings he would hardly have had time to answer the telephone, much less take time out to indulge an itching foot, in between the customers and the feed mixing in the back and making out orders for the salesmen due in the afternoon. But there is not that kind of rush any more at Billings Feed and Hardware, so my father has plenty of time to address himself, with complete concentration, to toe inspection or string collecting or just about any other little diversion that might show up during the course of a day.

I can see him peering down just a little more closely at his foot now, considering it further. He thinks he might try a little iodine on it, too.

He opens one of the side drawers of the desk — one of the many that have grown cluttered in recent years — and searches among the Pepsi-Cola empties and old fried-pie wrappers and faded invoices until he finds his iodine. He looks down closely again as he touches the little glass applicator to the cracks in his toes. The iodine hurts, and he draws in his breath with a little hissing intake.

"Sussss, dad *gum* the luck. *Ummmh!*" He winces and shakes his head a little at the pain.

My father hears the front door of the store opening. He closes up the iodine bottle and gives a glance to his foot before straightening up in his swivel chair to look out over the desk and see who has come in.

It is Frances Bouldin, the Negro woman who buys a quarter's worth of lime and a dime's worth of pigeon grit. As usual, she is carrying a couple of paper bags.

"Hello, Frances," my father says, looking at her briefly before turning back to survey his foot a final time. "Be with you in a minute."

"Oh, I ain't mindin, Mistah Billins. I been to town already this mornin and I'm just triflin now."

Frances generally fluctuates between two basic moods — she's either rather jaunty and carefree, or preoccupied with some personal gloominess: like she was, say, when her parakeet froze the very night after taxi fare went up to a quarter. Today she seems untroubled.

She soon notices my father's vacant sock and shoe beside the desk.

"Oh Mistah Billins, you havin feet troubles too? My, there's nothin meaner sometimes than just ole *feet* trouble." She hugs her two paper sacks a little closer, swaying, then cocks her head to one side in order to get the full scope of feet trouble in better focus. "Sometimes, I tell you, my feets get to hurtin me so bad downtown I just want to stand in that sidewalk and bawl like a *baby*. And I bet this ole feed store gets you' feet the same way."

My father has his shoe on and rises from the swivel chair, clumping about experimentally to test the feeling in his doctored foot. He puts away the Dr. Scholl's powder in a desk drawer, stands by the desk to shuffle a paper or two, then turns to the cash register on the counter. He makes a notation on the back of a check blank about something he just remembered he wanted to take home after work.

Frances is reading items on the For Sale blackboard when he finally steps behind the counter.

"Need some lime today, Frances?" my father asks.

Still reading, Frances answers in a vacant, singsong way: "Yassir, Mistah Billins, I believe I'll take about a quarter's worth."

I can see my father moving on down behind the counter toward the warehouse door — not leaving Frances with any noticeable rudeness, not moving with obvious, unlistening abruptness, but with just a little grimness and a slight favoring of his stinging right foot. He has never felt any deep fondness for Frances: back in the days when the store still delivered she would call up for fifty cents' worth of rabbit pellets and want it delivered "by five o'clock for *sure*, Mistah Billins, 'cause you know I *always* tries to be reg'lar in my feedin."

Frances stands firmly holding her two paper bags. Her small rimless glasses, that somehow are always glinting, blot out her eyes like a pair of little silvery shields. My father goes through the middle door to the back warehouse part where we used to keep feed. He fishes around in an old wooden grain barrel full of papers and trash and finally shakes the dust off a crumpled paper sack; then, after getting a scoop from a nearby empty bin, he weighs out a quarter's worth of lime on the scales. He lets fall a little extra jag of lime for good measure and then twists the neck of the sack. He calls:

"You need some pigeon grit today, Frances?"

Frances always ends up buying pigeon grit when she comes to the store, but she never asks for it first. My father generally has to bring it up.

"Yassir, I suppose since I'm already in I might as well get some. How much is it a pound today, please?"

"Six cents," answers my father. It has been six cents forever, I think — it was six cents even when I worked at the store back in the forties. Frances knows that the chances of its still being six cents are pretty strong, but she always inquires just on principle.

"I suppose I'd just better have me a dime's worth today, then, Mistah Billins."

My father reaches down into the trash barrel for another sack, finds one, and give it a shake to clear away the dust.

My father has owned Billings Feed and Hardware since 1937, and over the years it has seen, by and large, some pretty good days. It weathered several long, severe droughts, lasted out the war and family hospital bills. It never made my father prosperous but it made money enough to feed and clothe us all and to send my brother and me off to college. It hung on stubbornly and unspectacularly in the face of competitors who would open up in town, flourish mightily for a while, and then for some reason sicken and die or else settle down to being just ordinary business rivals.

I guess the store hung on for the simple reason that most people found out they liked to trade with my father. Many times,

I know, they would continue to come up to the store even when they might be able to get feed cheaper some place else for a while or, in the case of out-of-towners, even buy closer home. I suppose that over the years people came to believe that Fred Billings was that institution called A Good Man, and after they got that idea in their heads they just went on doing business with him, period. They found that he was honest, that he could be counted on to go out of his way to help a person, that he was never mean-acting or short-tempered. Too, he was a kind of amateur vet, in a way, and there were lots of times when someone with a bloated cow or sick chickens would phone up and say, "Fred, I got me a bunch of old Plymouth Rocks that are just drooping around, not laying, their old combs flopped over and turned bilious-looking: what d'you think I ought to do with them?" And my father, after giving his little preparatory, professional-sounding throat clearing, would ask a question or two further and then advise the caller about what ought to be done.

Sometimes when I get to thinking back on the pre-Frances Bouldin era and all the things the store used to be for people — for my father when he was making out of that big old warehouse not just a business but a way of life; for the ranch and town folks who came by to socialize as much as to buy feed; for me when I was growing up and helping out there in the afternoons — I can't help but hate it the way it is now. It's gone down hill so badly in the past few years I don't even like to go around it any more. It's just actually painful for me to look around at the empty, dusty shelves up front in the office and hardware part, or to walk around in the back warehouse where all the mashes and grain and hay used to be. Nowadays my father stores things for people instead of selling feed: he still keeps a few dabs of things for the likes of Frances Bouldin who just need a dime's worth of this or a quarter's worth of that, but his income now comes from renting out little squares of space in the warehouse for people who want to store air conditioner units or cold drink cases or maybe old furniture. The last time I was in the store there were even some old bedsprings and a couple of rusted Maytag washing machines.

I wish the store could have kept on the way it was before my father lost his grip, or whatever it was, and began to back off into old age. Some of the relatives think it was his back operation that threw him for a loop: the VA doctors down in Houston scared him up pretty badly about ever lifting anything again and so for a long time afterward he just kind of sat around, not re-ordering any stock, hardly even noticing how the customers were drifting away because they couldn't get what they wanted any more. Maybe it was just simply that, the shock of the opera-tion. Or maybe it was the last severe drought that came along about the same time and made a lot of people in the feed busi-ness uneasy and even put out of commission some of the best ranchers in the hill country. Maybe it was those things, and some others I don't even know about — things inside him, that only he knows — that caused my father almost overnight to take up the habits and thinking of an old man, and caused things around the store to go to staves.

That old tin-roofed, sparrow-nesting warehouse had a loveli-ness about it, a peaceful sun-shining-on-a-warm-board content-ment that made everybody who came there feel at home. Many an afternoon when I was working there I'd take a break and sit in the doorway on the steps, eating ice cream and watching the scenes around the block. Across the street to the west the sun would be catching itself in some of the tallest elms behind the bakery, haloing the trees and touching up the grass in a couple of vacant lots around; and now and then you could get a whiff from the bakery of pastries and fresh bread; and there would be a hum of some kind of saw going in the metal shop right next door — not loud, but just a pleasant, afternoon sound, seeming as though the man running the saw might even be taking a good little pleasure out of the sound and feel of his work as well as knowing that he was doing something honorable and constructive in the world.

And sometimes the man who ran the secondhand shop on the other side of the bakery would be standing with his hat on underneath the shadowing eve of his store front, trying out the rod and reel someone had left with him to sell. He always seemed to get a genuine pleasure out of that reel: he'd cast out into the dusty, unpaved street between our place and his, reeling back his line in little jerky stops and starts — the way you do when you're trying to fool a fish — and the lead weight on the end of his line bouncing along over the dusty rocks somehow rather sad and lonesomely. Sometimes he would stand there for nearly half an hour or more, just casting and recasting, as if knowing that was going to be the closest he would ever get to any actual fishing.

And over to the south of the store the Mexican kids would all be straggling up the tracks, coming home from school. There would usually be an open railroad car along the tracks, and the guys from the lumberyard in town would be unloading sheet-rock. They would have their shirts open in front, streams of sweat shining on their stomachs but all of them joking around, not at all killing themselves with the work, and always laughing loudest and making remarks while the prettiest Mexican girls passed on slowly up the tracks. And catty-corner from us was the Jersey Lilly beer joint, an old gray frame building with a high, square front and one lone hackberry tree outside the front door. For most of an afternoon there would just be one car or two parked in front and the occasional sound of some woman's high cackle in the big echoing hall, but when the painters and carpenters got off work about four-thirty or so the cars would begin to point in their noses all around the place and the jukebox would get going with all the slow, mournful hillbilly songs you ever heard.

Yes, when I get to thinking about it, there were lots of nice things about that old store. Back in the good days of the thirties and forties when I was growing up — when the sign was still freshly painted in big letters along the side of the building and my father had sometimes two hired hands working for him — I remember I liked to watch how the big vans from the roller mills in San Antonio and other places brought us our feed. They would come backing up slowly to one of the warehouse doors, the driver twisted part ways out the window of his cab, carefully jackknifing the van out of the street until the back end matched flush with the loading platform. Then the driver would let loose that big steaming sigh of his air brakes and he would lumber down out of the cab, taking off his black-billed driver's cap and mopping his big, white, sweating forehead with his bandana. He would walk very slowly to the front part of the store and leave the sweat-stained invoice with my father and go on back into the small bathroom we had in the warehouse. He'd relieve himself, take several good long drinks from the gray-enameled tin cup that always hung by the water faucet, and come out still mopping his sweating hands on his white apron. He'd take off his billed cap again and wipe off more sweat with the back of his arm and then go to the loading platform doorway and stand in the breeze to light a cigarette. He'd stand there a while, resting and smoking, looking across the street to see what was going on there, and then finally he'd go to the back of his van and undo the big doors and begin to unload out of the pleasant, feed-sweetened darkness of the van his shipment of grain and mashes. He would work for half an hour or more with his neat, well-balanced little loading truck, rolling his six-and-seven-feedsack-high stacks of cottonseed meal and wheat bran and laying mash across the splintery warehouse floor and dumping them effi-ciently row after row along the walls (sometimes those great stacks of feed grew so temptingly high that small boys, if not watched by their customer fathers, would climb up sack by sack until they could touch the rafters. They were huge mountain ranges of feed, slanting gradually downward from the walls like miniature Alleghenies sloping toward the sea: maize, oats, wheat, corn, hundreds of pounds of each, sack upon sack, each a separate mountain system, each distinctive: Oat Ridge, Barley Butte, Rabbit Pellet Hill . . . and occasionally the small-boys-turned-alpinists would make their way from stack to stack, leaping deep chasms made where stock had dwindled low, striding boldly along high pleasant plateaus of alfalfa and peanut and Johnson grass hay, inching their way across knee-skinning, rough Siberian flats of sulfur block salt: sometimes being able to navigate the entire main rectangle of the warehouse without once touching the floor).

During the good years some people came by as much to pass the time of day in the store as to buy feed. They felt comfortable sitting in one of the small, cane-bottomed chairs we had in front and looking out the south doorway down the railroad tracks. In summertime there was always a good breeze that swept up the long open clearing of the trackway into the store; it used to be people's favorite conversation opener. They'd rock back in their chair, maybe light up a cigarette, shove their hat back a little from their forehead, gaze down the tracks past the vacant lots and warehouses, and say to my father, "Fred, you've got the coolest place in town, right here."

And if there was a quiet two-o'clock lull in business, chances are the customer and my father would engage in the Great Feed Store Dialogue. My father, with his hat on, as always, would have stationed himself behind the counter just to the side of the cash register, his profile presented as a kind of offering of good listenership to the customer in the chair, his gaze directed vaguely, peacefully, and noncommittally somewhere in the neighborhood of the Burpee Seed Calendar on the south wall or the long crack beside it in the window glass. He was foremost a listener, an assenter, and that was what made the men who sat in the doorway comfortable, for they were usually talkers: small, sports-clothed retired colonels who found the informal atmosphere of the store to their liking since they had nothing more to do with their lives except to take care of their fine lawns and keep out red water for the hummingbirds and talk about their past military decisions; or wheezing, coughing, spitting old country men, barely able to make it up the front porch steps, who usually had spent most of their morning and afternoon across the street at the Jersey Lilly: tough, leathery but nevertheless worn-out old men, soon to die of cancer if they didn't cough their asthmatic lungs out first or fall into a ditch and freeze to death on their way home some night from a beer joint: old men who had known my father when he was a boy living out on a ranch and liked him after he grew up and would still walk halfway across town to buy fifteen cents' worth of rape seed from him rather than buy it from a fancy-dan new Purina man in their neighborhood.

On occasion, though, the chair would be filled by one of the successful ranchers in the area who would come clomping up the front steps, his big boots polished to a T, his face pink and shiny from his fresh barbershop shave, his khaki pants and shirt smooth over his big stomach and thighs and still creased right: he would spread out in the chair with his legs apart and chew on a match stem and occasionally spit out the door and then in the middle of some trifling, general conversation about weather would say abruptly, "Fred — what kind of price can you make me on a ton of range cubes?" And he'd spit again and chew on his match and look out the door while my father rustled around at his desk and found the back of an old envelope to figure on. If my father's price turned out to be all right, the rancher would slap his hands down hard on his thighs and hoist himself out of the chair and clomp on out the front door, hardly slowing down in passing to say, "All right, Fred, you go ahead and order me a ton and I'll send Joaquin in with the truck first part of next week," and down the wooden steps he'd go to his Buick, slamming the door hard and gunning out of the gravel and dust by the store to tend to his other business down the street.

(Those big income days, the ton of this, the carload of that: "Remember that $500 day, son?" my father recently asked me. I was at the store and somehow the conversation had turned to that Saturday back in the forties when all the first-of-the-month bills were being paid on time for once and when it had suddenly dawned on all of us that if business kept going as it had been up to three o'clock the cash register might surprise itself with a completely brand-new number by closing time. Customers were sometimes standing two and three deep during the afternoon and after any of us finished making a sale we would hurriedly lift up the lid on the cash register and see how far along we were toward $500. And it got to be a quarter to six and we were still $43 away from making it and dead tired — ready to close up and be content with being as close as we were — when an old man named Turner came driving up his box-square '20-something Ford and dug through his black coin purse until he found his monthly statement and then slowly thumbered out $52.75 from his watch pocket and slowly wadded up the receipt my father gave him and put it in his watch pocket and drove away).

It's nearly closing time at the store, and I can see my father sitting on a stool in one of the warehouse doorways, finishing up a little job he started a while ago. He has a kerosene rag in his hand and he is bending over a Maxwell House coffee can full of old nails. He wipes each nail thoroughly, cleaning away the rust. Every now and then he takes a bent nail and lays it on a wooden block he has nearby and taps it several times with his hammer to straighten it out.

A customer comes in, asking for a bushel of oats, and my father says he sure is sorry but he's out of oats right now. The man says he needs some to take home to a horse and asks where he could get some before six; my father says he might try the new place right down the street. My father doesn't rise from his bent-over, hammering position on the stool as he talks to the man. When the man leaves, my father turns back to his coffee can of nails. He scatters the nails about, searching out the ones that still need to be wiped clean. There are just a couple left. He pulls out his pocket watch and squints at it in the fading light of the doorway. There's still time to clean the last few before closing time. He puts his watch away and picks up his kerosene rag.

In the office the telephone is ringing but my father doesn't hear.

Heartland

1: *Rabbit, at Sundown*

🙵 ONCE, JUST AT DARK, a rabbit fell down and a man saw him. The man, a rancher, was seated behind an oak tree near a windmill in his pasture. He had been working on the mill that afternoon and had sat down to rest a few moments when the jackrabbit came scooting along a trail through a group of cedar trees. Daylight had almost completely faded and the rabbit was simply doing what it did many afternoons — come in to get water and nibble in the hay that was scattered around the mill for cattle. The rancher was looking off into space — not moving — so every-

thing seemed quite safe and ordinary to the rabbit. But just as he got clear of the cedar trees and into the open area around the mill, he saw the rancher looking straight at him. He braked, became confused, and fell, all within an instant, tripping over himself and his long feet in the dust. As he went down the rabbit looked across at the man — not with fear or concern for his safety but in simple amazement at what he, a wholly nimble and healthy rabbit, was allowing himself to do. He was down only a fraction of a moment, just long enough to know beyond doubt that he had truly fallen and there had truly been a witness — that he had not dreamed it all — and then he was up and gone, zigzagging in furious shame across the clearing and into a clump of shin oaks and out of sight.

II : *San Antonio Streets in Summertime*

DOWNTOWN, a thin bony-shouldered young man in a wrinkled white shirt is on the move along the sidewalk by the Greyhound bus station. His cigarette fumes at his side and the metal taps on his dusty black shoes click against the sidewalk. He is loose in the Big City, carrying his tender untried country-boy manhood the way he carries his cigarette — with an air of fierce negligence and unconcern. But it is no use, he gives himself away. His lean, trouser-flapped legs cut the hot noonday air too fiercely; they are like bony blades sharpened for combat. And as he crosses catty-corner from the bus station to a small bar across the street, his eyes shoot about him with too much of a furtive, protective scowl — looking too hard and not finding anything to see.

Off San Pedro Street, in a solemn old section of white two-story houses, a small window radio plays tunes from the 1940's. Behind the rusted screen, shadowed by magnolia trees, Woody Herman elegantly whines "I'm Glad There Is You" — his solo curling out to the sidewalk like cool spring waters and taking the edge from the hot afternoon.

On West El Paso Street diapered Mexican babies sit spraddle-legged under back yard chinaberry trees, playing with rocks and raising black eyes at the sound of footsteps beyond the green picket fence. Sweat and dirt streak their faces but they never cry. Occasionally one will stop playing long enough to investigate with his fingertip the brown mystery of his navel.

In Harlandale, in another back yard and under another chinaberry tree, a tubercular veteran of World War I sits with his shirt and shoes off, long hairs trailing beneath the nipples of his sunken white chest. He is seated in an old paint-peeled kitchen chair, watching two of his banty roosters fight in a shaded dusty clearing. He has tushes and a couple of black decaying front teeth; he shows them occasionally in a lopsided grin as one of the roosters demonstrates a little extra fury and spunk. A cigarette burns deeper nicotine stains against his fingers, and each time he takes a puff he coughs uncontrollably down between his spread-out legs. Afterwards he spits, looks at the stain on the ground, then raises up to watch the roosters fight some more.

On North St. Mary's, on the porches of run-down residential hotels and rooming houses, old men in round hats lean forward on their canes, gazing at shadows blotting the sidewalks and the bare grassless yards. Every now and then cars with double exhausts make the corner nearby and thunder past, hurling heavy flatulent sounds at the old men and the houses and the afternoon. As the cars fade out of hearing locusts in the tall hackberry trees along the sidewalks begin singing again, and the old bent-over men look toward them a while, vaguely. But they soon lose interest and gaze at things closer in—perhaps a gravy stain on one of their black shoes or a crack in the floor. They sit there, unmoving, the heavy strokes of idleness and old age carving them deeper into their porch swings and the summer afternoon.　⧫

III : *Old Maid*

W SHE WAS STANDING outside her house, examining a pear tree. A Sunday afternoon thundershower had just moved across town, and the leaves of the tree were still dripping on the yard. The woman was touching a pear carefully, feeling its slick body and the wetness on it.

After a moment she turned, stomped her houseshoes briefly against the sidewalk, and walked back to the front porch. She wiped the remaining mud from her heels on the scraper, then gathered her housecoat around her. After hesitating a moment, she decided to sit on the porch steps even though the boards were still damp.

She was forty years old and did not have a husband. Generally that was all right — being alone, not knowing the way women lived when there was a man with them in the house. But sometimes — like this moment, sitting on the porch following a Sunday afternoon rain — she felt bad about it.

The woman sat there, looking out at the street, watching the water drip from the pear leaves, and she tried not to think about how long it was from five o'clock in the afternoon until eight the next morning.

IV : *Ranch Woman on the Phone*

WAL, all finished with ya nap? . . . ah, hah . . . yas, wal, not much more'n a breath or two here either, not enough to help much, cert'nly . . . yas, wal . . . yas . . . unh, hunh . . . all through with ya cannin? . . . ah, hah . . . yas, wal, you're sure smart; I just din't think I'd do any this summer, just too lazy, I guess . . . (lazy chuckle here) . . . maybe that's it . . . yas . . . j'hear from Donnie Ray? . . . wal . . . wal . . . wal . . . wal I'll say . . . ah, hah . . . no, the baby had a little up-set and they thought they better not try to make this time . . . uh, hunh . . . yas, that's sure true, all right; there's lots of it goin around . . . yas, he gets two days off Labor Day, ya know, and they're plannin on comin up then . . . yas, wal, I think so, a-course (lazy laugh here) . . . ah, hah . . . ya still goin to Doctor Karrel? . . . yas . . . wal . . . wal . . . wal . . . well I de-clare . . . ah, hah . . . well I imagine so, unh-hunh . . . yas, wal I always thought so but didn't really know for sure, ya know . . . ah, hah . . . wal . . . wal, I guess I better letche go so I can go fix Weldon his coffee; he's got to run into Fred'icksburg this after-noon to see about some in-surance papers . . . wal, you do that . . . wal . . . (lazy chuckle here) . . . wal, we'll try to but no tellin when we'll break away . . . (short lazy chuckle) . . . 'n yawl try to come when ya can . . . wal-I-better-letche-go-now bye.

v : *Sally-from-the-country*

Ꙏ SHE WAS WHIPPING along through the open stacks of the San Marcos college library one warm September night, hot on the trail of Blasco Vincent Ibanez, when she rounded a corner in the Spanish literature section and ran full tilt into Tony Marmoset and his man-smell. This was the short, almost simian Tony of lush sideburns and swarthy features who instead of being born was evidently molded from some thick, quick-drying brown clay and his features then carved with hard strokes of a nail. This was the Tony who, as one awe-struck sophomore girl put it, had chiseled dimples.

Tony's habit was to get in an hour's worth of tennis before dark and then drop into the library without bothering to change from his athletic to his public smell. As he browsed in the close airless passageway of the stacks his body odor hung out from him a good yard or more. The smell, by anyone's standards, was a masterpiece of maleness.

When Sally bounced around the H-I corner of the Spanish literature shelf Tony turned slightly and permitted one sculptured eyelid to raise itself at her, lizardlike. He nodded briefly, closed his book over a finger to keep the place, and slowly withdrew his hairy belly from her path. His T-shirt and shorts did not meet at the waist and, as she squeezed past, his protruding cauliflower navel stared up at her like a fat man's blind yet knowing eye.

It was nothing more than this — a passing nod and a virile smell — that caused Sally-from-the-country to fall victim to the charms of Tony Marmoset. To some casual bystander she would have seemed none the worse for wear as she steamed on down toward her rendezvous with *Blood and Sand.* But had old shrewd friends been watching, they would have noticed immediate changes in Sally. They would have seen her add in dead mid-stride an extra fillip to the switch of her buttocks, as if she had suddenly shoved herself into overdrive. They would have noticed an unnecessary "sophisticated" tilt to her chin as she began searching the library stacks. They would have noticed too how she kept turning this way and that, allowing her long brown hair to split and slide around from shoulder to shoulder with a fluid, ball-bearing ease, like topsails being managed by a competent sailor during a suddenly arrived storm.

Now Tony's smell was offensive; this was incontestable, even to Sally. It was a potent mixture of body odor and stale sweat, stunningly emulsed in dead air. If Sally had been at all interested in saving herself from masculine destruction, she could have busied herself with any number of logical and feminine reflections — about how much of an animal a human being really is, especially a male; and how an ape or lion could certainly smell no worse in a library than Tony did in his white gym shorts and tennis shoes. But at 18, on a warm September night, Sally knew better than to bother with anything her nose might tell her. Years of reading farm magazines on lonely Saturday nights, years of vague longing as she lay by herself in her cold upstairs bed — they told her to stay away from any foolish dealings with her *nose*. The essential thing, the only thing, was that Tony and his man-smell constituted the most magnificent and shocking power she had ever run into. It made her feel weak.

She let her forefinger pause on the tops of books as she pulled them out partway, studied them, shoved them back. Little by artful little she managed to move toward Tony. She knew he was watching her over the top of his book: even though the Cary Grant chin was resting on the curling black hairs of his collarbone and the eyelids were drooped to half-mast, she knew he was looking — perhaps not hard, perhaps just routinely, but nevertheless, *looking*.

Sally tried her best to hold books provocatively, with the forefinger of her free hand poised efficiently at the top of the left-hand pages. She was perfectly aware that she had good legs, and as she casually lifted a bare heel out of her shoe she flexed the calf muscle of the leg hard. She held the heel free, then, as if absent-mindedly, let it slide down into the shoe again. She kept slipping the heel back and forth as she read: more skin to show, more skin not; more skin to show, more. . . .

She heard Tony snap his book shut and replace it on the shelf. Her heart stopped, there was silence, he started toward her, and she heard him asking her some routine get-acquainted question about "Spanish lit." She didn't hear exactly what he said for she was too busy thinking, joyously: "Thank God, I've got on the good brassiere."

VI : *Pilot*

AN AIRLINE PILOT and his shapely wife were taking an afternoon stroll down the shopping center mall. Everything about him suggested buoyancy, flight, a purely temporary attachment to earth; everything about her suggested solid comforts, womanliness, bed.

The pilot was not in uniform. He wore a short-sleeved white knit shirt, blue walking shorts, pale blue canvas shoes without socks. His hair—pewter-going-to-gray—was cast into iron waves; his moustache, a carefully trimmed and polished-looking wing, hovered lightly above his upper lip.

As he walked past the store windows the pilot pretended interest in diamonds, walnut furniture, clothes. He nodded gravely at floor lamps. But even as they stood paused in front of the shining display glass, considering luxuries, the pilot's tanned calf muscles were flexing smoothly — as if they were idling little body motors that could, at a moment's notice, send him aloft.

VII : *St. Anne of Dallas Mutual*

NOT QUITE VOLUPTUOUS but certainly eyesome and well-formed, St. Anne met all the requirements of a bathing beauty except openness and warmth. She was too cool, too passive, too *removed* — and had no instinct for self-demonstration. In the two years she worked as a secretary for Wilford Cody, she never once heated up his filing cabinets.

As she crossed and recrossed the tiles of Dallas Mutual Finance — passing right by Wilford's desk — her breasts never flapped or bulged in any kind of unseemly display. They existed quietly in their charming abundance, dozing within the snug caves of St. Anne's brassiere like smooth, elegant, domesticated animals.

Her legs, tensioned above high heels, had round jutting calf muscles that Wilford found beautiful to consider — but as objects of art. He knew that he might encounter them in the Smithsonian Institute above a small card labeled "Perfect Legs *secretarius americus*," yet he never seriously thought of them lying beneath the sheet of some fellow's bed.

St. Anne had a perfect Valentine's face, rounded and curved, and she always smelled deliciously of powder. When she smiled, perfect lips broke apart to reveal the perfect whiteness of perfect teeth. Yet she was not quite a pedestal goddess: she was alive and demonstrably human because on warm days there were little dark, blouse-staining half-moons under her arms. And sometimes she had fine beads of moisture beneath her eyes. Yet it always seemed to Wilford that her mortality was something she endured rather than enjoyed. She would have been much happier without the sweat, or the hair that she had to shave daily from her legs (— yet, since they were what mortality brought her, she succeeded in having the smoothest legs and creamiest underarms in town).

On those few occasions when Wilford was alone in St. Anne's presence — when she sat with him in her plush apartment, saying very little, gazing down into her lap — Wilford watched in a kind of quiet, sustained wonder, trying desperately to keep from breathing, or blinking his eyes, or doing any other kind of routine physical thing that might offend her. He sat in pure, direct awareness of her beauty, and considered all the things he would lay at her feet if he only knew how.

He wanted very much to gain her favor, yet, strangely, when he got near to her there was no wild heat, no strong primitive urge that drew him madly to her core. Indeed, whenever he did come close to losing self-control — and behaved with an unseemly ardor that caused St. Anne to frown her displeasure — Wilford always wanted to stuff his bothersome lust in a brown paper bag and throw it out the window. For St. Anne had that powerful feminine knack of making Wilford — indeed, all her suitors — want to leave her presence chastened, purified, and Just Good Friends.   ⋑

VIII : *Johnnie*

❦ IT WAS SATURDAY MORNING and he was bent over the piano in Mike's Friendly Tavern in Waco—motionless, his body frozen, his hands on the keys. Was he waiting, thinking? At first you wondered. Then a customer called to him from the other end of the bar.

"Hey, Johnnie, play "It Had To Be You."

For a moment there was no reaction, then Johnnie unfroze. He swung around on his piano stool, his thumb and forefinger held together, touching, making a big letter O.

"Caaaat!" Johnnie cried to the customer, and swung his sign of approval broadly in the air. Then quickly, hurriedly, he began his routine. Out came the comb: he made it fly through his hair — with jerks, with torturous, circuitous movements — before returning it deftly, like a vaudeville magician, to his back pants pocket. Down went the hands, then instantly they were brought back up again, knotted and pressed against his chest. Down they went still another time, spread and rigid over the keys, waiting. He looked ready now, he was going to play. But no, the hand to the back pocket, the comb again. . . .

"Here you go, Johnnie, compliments of that gentleman right over there." The bartender leaned across the counter and put the glass of beer on top of the piano. He pointed down the bar to a customer who was watching.

A quick swing around, the squeak of the stool, and — Caaaat! Johnnie made his sweeping sign, his letter O. Then both hands went out together, cupped — as though about to trap a small animal or bird — and they surrounded the glass of beer. Johnnie drained it quickly and with both hands returned the glass to the top of the piano with exorbitant, apologetic carefulness — patting the rim once and waiting a second, as though to see if the glass might accidentally move or come alive. And then, as though suddenly remembering the request for the tune, as though far behind schedule, Johnnie swept his comb through his hair, threw his hands down where they could hover over the keys, forcibly hunched his shoulders, and began beating a loud hollow preparatory four with his right tennis shoe against the wooden platform.

The regular customers in the bar smiled for a while at Johnnie, yelled songs to him, bought him beers, then gradually settled into their own talk. But the drop-ins, the uninitiated — they sat at the counter and stared: at Johnnie's sun glasses, with one red lens and one green; at his tennis shoes with the sides cut out and the little toe of each foot showing; at the dark freckles splotched like old iodine on his face and arms; at the sound of the muffled, husky voice coming through his toothless mouth; at the jerks, the twists, the sudden freezes of hand or arm or shoulder; at the comb flying repeatedly through the shaggy red hair.

Sometimes after Johnnie finished a piece he held his hands on the keys for a long moment. He would draw the fingers into the palms, then bring both hands straight back to his shoulders, flipper-like; finally he would drop his head away and cover his face with his hands. And he would begin to talk. Only the customers sitting close to the piano heard him. It was as though he were talking to an invisible partner there on the stool beside him: "Oh," he would say, "I feel so sad today I think I will have to cry," and he would finger a button on his shirt. "Yes! Nothing else to do; I must cry." He would freeze there, bent over, his hands covering his face. Then with a sudden "Oh!" he would unfreeze, throw out his arms, jerk himself up straight, and bring one hand flat against the side of his face. "No! Not cry! Of course not; I must play! My God, there is too much to cry about . . . I would never stop." He would nod his head, agreeing with himself sadly. "No, I would never stop." And giving his whole body a good cleansing shake, he would hunt for his comb in his back pocket and peer briefly at the top of the piano to see if there was any beer in his glass.

Sometimes after that he would play a long series of tunes very softly, hitting the right notes, keeping the proper beat — and doing it despite all the exaggerated movements of his elbows and shoulders and knees.

Yet at other times he seemed to catch a glimpse of some old private nemesis and set out to chase it and beat it to death on the keyboard with his big cracked hands. With his tennis shoes stomping hard, his head hanging loose and wild below his shoulders, his body jerking and swaying, he was like a perverse and nearly ruined human machine — one with emotional bearings worn out and mental threads rubbed smooth but still able to function, still able to work the tireless, avenging pistons in his hands. ⋙

IX : *Young Bride*

   IT IS WINTER NOW. There are few leaves left on the trees and little music left in her soul. She stands in her apartment house doorway, looking out at the dry grass in neighboring yards. It is mid-morning in January and there is almost no sound to hear — a dog maybe, a few slow-moving cars.

She tries to understand why it is that days have such a strange blend of silence and stillness now. She does not remember meeting such days before. Why, they used to turn about her so easily, in such a pleasant, inevitable way, they were like seats on a ferris wheel. She did not used to think at all about *days*. . . .

As she stands in her long, vacant-stared moment of thought, she remembers the breakfast dishes that are sitting on the kitchen table, the bundle of dirty clothes on the bathroom floor. She remembers, too, why she is paused there in the doorway. She looks down past her married-life robe and married-life slippers to the morning newspaper on the steps.

Inside her body is a child. She thinks of it as she mounts the narrow stairs to her apartment. She thinks of it and then of her husband — that young man whose name is on the mailbox, whose name will be given to the child — and after she has walked along the silent carpet she finds herself at her apartment door. She pauses, her hand on the knob, and with words so loud in her mind that she is sure she is screaming, she thinks: What has *happened* to me? Where in the world have I gone? Who are these people that are taking over my life? Holding on to the knob, she does not cry. She makes no sound in the hallway. She looks down at the bulge of her robe and goes inside the apartment to do the dishes.   ⋑

x : *Clark*

TALL, BROAD-SHOULDERED, slim-hipped, he rises at the first scrape of the fiddle and half-dances himself over to a girl four tables away. He does not look directly at her while offering his hand: he correctly assumes her acceptance, her pleasure. Even after the girl has pushed her chair aside and fitted into the waiting curve of his arm, he keeps his handsome face turned away — locked in profile — and sweeps her masterfully away into the circle of pumping, gliding dancers.

Everyone knows Clark at the Highway Inn: telephone lineman by day, honky-tonk whirling dervish by night. Everyone knows the head of carefully neglected hair, the polished lineman's boots, the long black comb jutting from the back pocket of his denims.

Everyone knows, too, that his name isn't Clark — that some cigar-chewing buddy had first tagged him with "Hollywood" and then with "Clark" and that the second nickname had stuck. Yet Clark takes the razz in stride, for he is perfectly aware of how he stands at the Highway Inn. A ladies' man, sure, but hellfire — can't he drink and cuss and stay-out-all-night-and-still-go-to-work-the-next-morning with the best of them?

After each dance Clark deposits his partner at her table — lets her slide from his arms toward the chair — and returns to the waiting whiskey bottle at his table. He does not bother much with chitchat, but as he pours himself a drink he winks at a hurrying waitress, nods to a couple of pals. Then, stretching out his long slender legs and placing the paper cup full of Jim Beam at his side, Clark gazes out serenely across the milling crowd. ⋑

XI : *Initiation at Mesa Verde*

W IN THE BIG PARKING LOT of the Lubbock shopping center a dozen or so young boys, all with the same expensive headdresses and same expensive beaded moccasins, were deep into their dance. It was a dance of initiation and they were in various stages of bending over and rearing back — some beating small drums, some shaking amulets on their legs and wrists, all making high, boy-fierce cries. They were a tribe of Suburban Indians, each one a clean-cut prospect for a Suburban brave.

Down the way from the initiation area a big, heavy-moving man in khakis and a straw hat was keeping a little troupe of Shetland ponies walking along in a slow circle, giving twenty-five cent rides to the children of the shoppers. The ponies were separate from each other but were linked by lightweight chains to a small machine in the middle.

It was a typical day at Mesa Verde Shopping Center, another pastoral Saturday afternoon on the asphalt with real-life horses and young Indian warriors from Scout Troop 137: a nice, tame wildwest show for the customers. As the crowd of parents and onlookers gazed out from the mall beside J. C. Penneys, the Shetlands walked around and around in their circle, each spirit-less, each following the white tail of the Shetland in front. The big man in khakis and straw hat walked beside them in the sun, steadying a child here and there, wiping his forehead constantly with his red handkerchief. The children rode contentedly, with great seriousness; a few of them smiled at their mothers in the sidewalk shade.

Who can say what caused the dark Shetland to break loose from his chain? Perhaps he was just moving slowly along, dozing, doing what he had done a hundred or thousand times before, when suddenly he was awakened and frightened by one of the braves yelling in his dance of the Sun and Moon. And perhaps some instinct of flight was naked in the pony for an instant and his rearing back in alarm was just enough to snap some worn rope or buckle. Whatever the cause, the Shetland that found himself free bolted from the circle of ponies and started to drag his small screaming rider by one caught shoe out across the asphalt.

... How meekly the drum beats died away, how quickly the bucking, plunging arms and legs of the young Indians fell into stillness. And their headdress feathers became curiously straight — erect and frozen as ears of frightened rabbits in a field — when the big man in sweating khakis began to run, hatless, across the parking lot, yelling at the Shetland pony with its dangling rider and dangling chain.

Home

In the 1930s and 1940s

1 : Summer (Ages 3-8)

❦ I LIVE INTIMATELY with the earth — with the warmth of rocks and the dampness of shadowed dirt, with the lightbrownness of fallen oak leaves and the many small wiggling feet of sowbugs under porches, with dry grass in the cuffs of my pants, with boards grown soggy in rotting picket fences, with sunlight shining on a smooth rock wall, with woodpiles and the damp early-morning wetness soaking into the live oak bark.

I am one-with-weeds, one-with-the-ground. A shadow slanting from a roof makes me feel good; an ant crawling along a trail gives me pleasure.

I am a child of trees, nurtured by shade, by huge bark-bodies. ➤

—Jim Taylor comes up the hill, grinning, not exactly hanging his head but sort of having it over to one side, sort of sneaky-looking and sly. He lives down at the Taylor place by the creek and everyone in the neighborhood knows he is not quite right in the head but no one knows if he is dangerous or not. Some say he starts fires in vacant houses.

The whole Taylor bunch is strange. Old Man Taylor is always out on his cot during the summertime, sitting in the shade of the chinaberry tree in his undershirt, with long white wispy hairs curling out from his chest. He was a good stone mason once — he built the fish pond and bird bath in our front yard — but now he just sits around, smoking his Kite cigarettes under the chinaberry tree and calling out to Jim, his favorite of the seven children.

Jim, that strange, slouching, steadily moving figure: he comes up the hill every morning with his pocketful of matches, slinging

his head, not paying any mind to the old man back on the worn
canvas cot who keeps calling after him: "Jim . . . *Ji-immmm* . . .
goddamn you, Jim." He passes in the street beside our fence,
headed toward the school buildings and town. . . . Where does
he go each day? To set fires? To grin and sneak around up in
Hill Crest, where people live in fancier houses?

Annie Mae, Jim's oldest sister, is helping Mother clean the
kitchen as Jim goes by; I can hear her sweeping while I look
through the picket fence. I watch Jim's bare feet move through
the gravel and dust, watch him jerk his head as he talks to himself and grins. I watch him turn a couple of times and grin wider
— at the voice from below the hill, maybe; at the matches in his
pocket; at some soft, pleasing thing he keeps hidden there in his
mind. I watch him stick out his tongue and lick the side of his
mouth as he slings himself forward out of sight.   🍃

*—There are eruptive sweeps of wind in early summer that make
a person stop what he is doing and gape. Rising out of nowhere,
full of awkward vitality, they spill blusteringly through the trees
like wild flocks of big-winged birds. They fill the air; then,
without warning, they disappear as suddenly as they have come,
leaving the trees and the dry roadside shaken and still. They are
like demonic forces left over from Indian days and legends:
Thoughts-in-wind.*   🍃

— neighbor child: He comes running around the corner of his
house, whipping his leg with his hand as he imagines he would
his horse, and yelling DUN DA LA RUN, DA LUN DARRUN. DRRRRRNNN.
He gallops across half the yard, greets the grass with a gradual
collapse, and lies sprawled next to the water hydrant. He rests
there, contented and tired of playing. He finds a redbug bite
and picks at it. He lies still, looking up at the sky, as if listening to
things there. Then, after a while, he gets up and walks rather
soberly around the corner of the house.   🍃

— On certain summer Sundays my companions are not other boys, or relatives, or books; they are riverbank weeds and strong yellow grasshoppers and small islands of gnats that revolve mindlessly in the air as I stare ahead at the circles spanning out from my bobbing cork. They are the pleasantness of the river, and the deep sense of trees, and silence, and the summer afternoon.

I am there by the river and the fish are in the water and my father is down the bank from me just out of sight, holding his pole and patiently smoking his cigar. I am standing there, watching my cork dip a little, grow still, dip again, grow still, dip once more. I am standing there, watching my cork, as the earth turns silently, as a cow bawls in a field nearby, as my father breaks wind, as leaves drift by in the current.

Waiting for the unseen perch to swallow my unseen worm, I gaze outward and I think no significant thoughts. I am only minimally me, along the river bank. I am part of the sycamore shade, part of the grass under my feet, part of the July afternoon. I am merely an extension of my fishing pole, and I am happy. ⋺

—*A rancher drives home in the late afternoon. At five o'clock he is through with town for another week and is heading back to his ranchhouse on the familiar, curving road. A grandson sits in the back seat, reading a funny book. In front the rancher's wife sits looking ahead toward suppertime.*

The car moves steadily along. Deer stop grazing in the roadside and, making high arcs, cross the fence into pastures of cedar and post oak trees. As the road curves further to the west the sun comes strongly into the rancher's window, against the deep, red-leather creases of his face. He pulls the brim of his hat lower and squints a little as the sun floods across the land. ⋺

— wickes street: It is a bare-ribbed glory road for the Creekers below the hill — for the housepainters and carpenters and beer joint waitresses who live in the little frame houses along Mason Creek and raise rabbits and bantam roosters and go to dances on Saturday night at the Big Drive-In.

Wickes Street: rocky and dusty and narrow and straight. It means barefooted children and old cars up on blocks and rusting junk and the thin white caliche dust that drifts into the oak trees of the yards in May and stays there until the September rains.

In other neighborhoods people are Methodist and Episcopalian and own ladies' dress shops and grocery stores and have their picture in the paper on Thursday because they are in the Kiwanis Club minstrel or have completed twenty-five years in the First State Bank. But along Wickes Street they are Baptist and Holy Roller and Church of the Nazarene and the only time they get their picture in the paper is when one of them catches a thirty-pound catfish on a trotline in the Guadalupe.

Wickes Street mean the cursing fat women of the Turner family, sitting in the screenless doorway of their one-room shack beside Mason Creek – raising fat illegitimate children and smelling very bad and looking out across the long sewage pipe that crosses the flat as they goddamn the world. . . . It means the Quinlan family and the tribe of small Quinlan boys who appear year after year at neighborhood doors, begging for milk in their high, thin, catlike voices – their smaller, dirtier-faced Quinlan sisters standing beside them: all of them barefooted and in wrinkled, faded, dirty clothes, all of them with the same Quinlan blank expression, same pale vacant blue eyes, same streaks of drying mucus running down from snub Quinlan noses.

II : *Fall (Ages 9-11)*

ELEMENTARY SCHOOL trips at midday: the class is in a long line, trailing down past my house to the creek. All of us are so short, so miniature – so *minor*, all things considered – yet so stunningly complete, so fantastically equipped even now with senses and memories. We sit in a picnic-circle, absorbing the feel of Mason Creek while we eat. We are lieutenant colonels and chemical engineers and lesbians and bread truck drivers and housewives and livestock judges, but we do not know that yet. We are merely fourth-graders on a lark, eating our sandwiches and drinking our chocolate milk through straws and being very small and tentative under the trees.

— I gather up the trash — newspapers, cereal boxes, the odds and ends that accumulate in the house every day — and burn it down by the garden. I strike a match and hold it to the edge of the *San Antonio Light* and then watch as the flame curls the edge of the newspaper and spreads in a growing little wedge of fire and smoke. I see the paper grow dark-yellow, then brown, then suddenly turn black and begin to lift apart in fragments and drift upward from the trash pile in waves of heat and float into the trees of the vacant lot behind the chicken house.

I enjoy being there under the morning sun, with the heat of the flames hard against my face. It is pleasant to punch the hissing cardboard boxes with my broken rake handle and flip open a smoldering *Ladies' Home Journal* so that the pages jump into flame.

I do not think about anything during this little moment of intensity. I do not wonder about the lines of print that are being destroyed so casually by the fire. I am not impressed by the fact that words — even these ordinary ones of the *San Antonio Light* — can exist one moment and not the next. I am not shocked to see that the reality of the newspaper is altered, within seconds, to the reality of the thin black flakes rising up to the trees.

I do not think about Absolutes there at the trash pile. I am a lover, not a thinker — a lover of days, feelings, sensations, life.

— Home from school, I sit at the kitchen table and listen to the sounds of noon: limbs scraping against the roof; the Chuck Wagon Gang wailing from a neighbor's radio; my fork knocking idly against my plate.

Through the front windows I see the trees in our yard, their big limbs hanging down, and I think of how they will remain there after I go back to school — how they will stand, patiently, through the one, two, and three o'clock hours, mildly waving their arms to the wind, the afternoon, the world.   ⋙

—*Women, once young, once high-school girls (with their skin soft and clear and only their knees rough-wrinkled as they sat on the school lawn at noon, their hair blown a little in an October breeze, smiling, laughing, tossing grass at the boys who sat cross-legged with them in their lazy circle): these young girls, once sixteen, now stand on Saturday afternoon with their children at their side, in Reiser's Variety Store, their faces still pretty but lining deeply with age. They are ranchers' wives, come to town from Mountain Home and South Fork and the Divide to do their weekly shopping. They are wives and mothers and are growing older. Crow's-feet pull strongly at the corners of their eyes; extra flesh pads their faces. Their youthful prettiness is being puffed and stretched and distorted.*

They stand there in the aisle as they will stand twenty years from now — greeting high-school friends who will still be trying to find the pretty girl of sixteen in the woman with gray hair.

. . . Time passing in Reiser's store; women smiling out pleasantly through their wrinkles.   ⋙

— *sundays at doug's:* In the afternoon after dinner my cousin Worth and I open the unpainted pasture gate behind the rock garage and walk down the long slope to the creek. The October sun is warm on the ground and the curving pasture road is pleasant to follow through the mesquites. Beyond the creek we walk along a goat trail into the cedars and Spanish oaks of Kensing Hill. Near the top of the hill we stop to push big rocks into ravines and watch them roll through the dark leaves and underbrush; we listen as they gather speed and begin to crash beautifully through the lower trees at the foot of the hill. When we finally reach the top where the Spanish daggers grow we look out to the windmill beside my uncle's house, and the lots and barns, and as we stand there we smell the fresh cool air as it comes to us from across the valley.

On the way down we stop for a while at the creek. We look at the wide leaves of the sycamores lying on the smooth white rocks of the creek where it has gone dry, and at the minnows circling in the shallow pools. The cows far down the bank raise their heads from the grass and stare at us as we throw sticks into the water and yell — just to be yelling — into the deep country stillness.

After eating four o'clock chocolate cake with the grownups we gather up stray hair tonic bottles and set them up on the fence posts of the big grain field west of the house. We chunk rocks at them until we get tired, then wander about in the clearing until it gets nearly dark.

Sometimes we climb onto the rock water tank beside the garden and walk around the edge of it while the sun goes down. As we watch the hills grow dark we can hear lone sheep beginning to bleat from the ridges north of the house.

Worth never wants Sundays to end. After Daddy finally calls out to me that it is time to go, and while we begin to put things into the car, Worth goes over to the big mesquite tree beside the garage and jabs at it slowly with his pocketknife. He still has his faded cotton shirt buttoned at the neck, and he looks sad.

Daddy starts the car and my uncle Doug stands there at the front window, barefooted and in his undershirt. He and Daddy have their final words about crops and weather and feed while Mike, Doug's collie, circles around in front of the car with his big tail flaring in the beam of the headlights.

We finally ease away into the clearing, everyone saying goodbye. As I look back I can see Worth standing in the darkness of the big mesquite, his head down, still jabbing at the tree with his pocketknife. ❧

— A neighbor woman in a bright yellow dress walks past our house, coming from town, and when she passes through the shade of a live oak tree she enters a stretch of suspended time: Her yellow dress emerges and disappears, emerges and disappears, as she passes beneath the limbs of the huge shadowing tree. For a moment she is time-become-sensual: a lazy flow of color and shade, an exquisiteness under sun and oak. . . . ❧

III : *Winter (Ages 12-14)*

❦ PLACING THE NEWSPAPER PICTURE of Betty Grable on the ground, I grab the chinning bar and begin to chin myself in our side yard. I pull myself toward the bar and then look down at the picture, at Betty Grable's legs — letting the curious new sexual delight begin to happen to me. As I tighten my arm muscles and wriggle upward, the muscle strain becomes nicely acute at my crotch. I begin to bend my knees and pull up my legs, all the while trying to look *even closer,* more intently, at the picture, trying to create another dimension of Betty Grable excitement that will make my leg-raising and muscle-straining and crotch-pulling bring about more of the strange, exciting stimulation that I have discovered.

. . . I hide the picture under rocks in the back yard. Days, weeks later I uncover it: There she is, still Betty Grable, but with her thighs and legs now moist and full of sowbug holes. ❧

— The sun at five o'clock, and the light from it moving across the grass of our front yard. Everything simply . . . *is,* yet in such depth that reality seems heightened — more real than reality can be. For the five o'clock silence is absolute silence. And the front yard trees and the bicycle and the side yard gate and the flagstone walk — they are also absolute, relating to nothing beyond themselves. They are embalmed in silence, in the cool air, in the terrific presence of light streaming against them and over them and around them from the sun in the west. It is like the moment just before an August storm, when trees become more green than green against the strange backdrop of sudden summer darkness.

The silence of the universe is deeply in the trees, in the land. It is the silence that dinosaurs heard as they looked up from their grazing and stared out into the ferns.   ⋑

— I sit round-headed and slender-necked in the junior high school band, blowing earnest whole notes into my music folder. I create long, moist, mournful buzzings and moos that I hope will grow more stately and dignified as I keep practicing. My hero is Tommy Dorsey and I have listened to him play "Marie" and "Song of India" and "I'm Getting Sentimental over You" on the record player so I know how a trombone is supposed to sound.

Thus I keep striving. At 2:30 in the afternoon I reach my foot out to the spit valve and release the gathered saliva and I try once more to shape whole-note magic in the bass clef.   ⋑

— *Suddenly there are ice-covered trees in the pastures as ranchers drive home from town in December. At three o'clock the limbs of the trees are white and brittle, with thousands of branches stiffly encased in winter strangeness. . . . Old oaks — awesome, private — are far from God's heaven yet overnight they have felt His mysterious touch and have become straight-jacketed by still another of the world's wonders.*

It is cold and quiet, and the pasture-stillness is interrupted only by the random crack of a heavy branch falling; by a tire humming past on the road; by sheep calling from the rocky flats.   ⋑

—Toys at Christmas, taken out onto yellow-grass yards along

Wickes Street. The fresh red paint of the croquet balls, and dump trucks, and rubber-tipped arrows. The voices of boys running and playing. The Christmas Day quietness in the neighborhood. The cars pulled up into dirt driveways and onto the grass. The bare day and the bare yards and the bare, breezeless air. The shadows coming early, in midafternoon. The dust stirred occasionally in the streets as pickups roar past in second gear.

And within the small frame houses, the men and their families: electricians and highway department workmen and garage mechanics and their loud-laughing wives and hair-lipped daughters. ⟫

— Mrs. Weingarten of Weingarten's Garage, quietly large in her unchanging gray sweater and dark dress, presiding efficiently over ledgers and auto parts. She is the Madame Defarge of Kilgore Street, waiting for . . . what: perhaps some final easing of a personal pain. She looks up, sees, and never smiles. She writes many figures daily in her plump, feminine hand; she listens to talk about generators and burnt valves as if it were Lutheran doctrine. On cold winter days, when the mechanics come in to warm their hands at the office heater, she notes their presence, questions them briefly, continues to record neat figures at her rolltop desk. ⟫

—Winter days, warm at midmorning with a pale sun out. Days with the quietly moving river nearby, the glint of sun on bare cypress limbs, grasses dry and brown along the bank.

A moodiness growing, with the long afternoon hours speaking of time silently passing and ordinary lives being privately lived. . . . A stillness in the neighborhoods, with sounds blending into the air the way the stars blend into the daytime sky. Back doors shut on side streets and they are like pistol shots, for the silence is not mere silence: it is a huge, sharp-edged waiting, a readiness, a rich unfolding of static December hours.

On the edge of town glossy leaves of oak trees burn with a mild light. Sunshine touches the thousands of individual green leaves, and all along the roadside the trees are full of shining white fire.

. . . There is no pain like the pain of such days — the pain of pleasant noon warmth and quiet river air; of roadside mailboxes standing in shadows; of many cedar trees on the sides of hills and white caliche gulleys slashing starkly down. It is the pain born of solitude, of cool breezes moving across wire fences into wide, brown, late-evening fields, of gradually coming dusk, of yellow lights coming on in the windows of frame houses along narrow country roads. ⊰

— For us, in our town, there is no involvement in the outside world because there *is* no outside world. We get newspapers and magazines, yes, and people we know talk about other places. Relatives come to visit neighbors along the street — from Arizona and Oregon and Minnesota — but their names are simply names you could read in a book. To us they are not believable people.

You see, it is only our town, and the hill country, and the towns and places just on the edge of the hill country, that are genuine. For this is where we live — where we have our daily community of lives. All the happenings of people in town, the seasons of the year — they are ours. They do not belong to a greater whole because we *are* the whole. . . . A baby who cries in the house down the street is not just any baby — it is the baby of *that* house and *this* street and *our* town.

January following December, the March wind blowing, the daily sun rising and setting — such things are too strongly with us to belong to a larger world. . . . Kansas City? It exists, perhaps, but it is not real. ⊰

IV : *Spring (Ages 15-17)*

🔥 THERE IS A SQUARE FISHPOND in our front yard, and although it is inviting and serviceable it never has any fish in it. All I can see is a mass of water lilies, a few large rocks, occasionally some moss. Yet it does not bother me that we don't put fish in our fishpond. I accept that square of lilies as being our manner of doing things: the reality of what is, is stronger than the logic of what should be.

I have the same feeling about the garden. I look at it down below the house — a narrow, weed-bordered strip next to the cow lot — and I know that with its little dab of onions and tomatoes and squash it is not big enough or successful enough to count as a proper garden, yet I never feel that I should be ashamed of it. It is so strongly ours, so much a part of us and the way we live, that I would no more try to disown it than I would try to disown myself.

Every broken-down gate, every rusting piece of tin half-buried in the sudan patch, every spider web and chicken dropping — they are part of me, of us, and I have no reason to believe that they would be any different if we suddenly started ordering the circumstances of our lives straight from heaven. ⇒

— On the main street of town you can see the same familiar people almost every Saturday. You see ranchers in their Stetsons and boots as they stand on the corner beside Schmerbeck's dry goods store. You see the hand of a smiling insurance agent forever raised shoulder high as he walks briskly to his midmorning coffee at the Milam Hotel Coffee Shop. He crosses the street, ever so polite and mannerly, but the ranchers do not truly respond, do not trust his too-quick-heartiness, his thick-soled, thick-edged shoes, his too-small, city-man's hat with its neat red feather. . . . You see dogs in the back of worn-out pickup trucks — border collies, mostly — waiting for lone old women in blue jeans to come down the post office steps and climb back into the pickup cabs and drive with old-woman independence and slowness down the city streets and out the Turtle Creek or Goat Creek or Cypress Creek Road to their small country places among the live oak trees. . . . You see a man with wide suspenders, starched white shirt, and a cigarette in a cigarette holder standing with a kind of Roman self-assurance beside a parking meter, looking out from the sidewalk toward the steadily passing cars and the yellow awning of Penneys Store: a man curiously out of place with his lack of hail-fellow air, with his cufflinks and rimless glasses and Southern gentleman suspenders. He is an outlander of some sort, a loner come obscurely into town — a middle-aged watcher of the streets who is fastidious and independent and strangely contained. . . . You see a young Negro woman dressed in nurse's aide white, and as you look you record the fact — without thinking it and certainly without using the word *Negro* because in the seventeen years that you have lived you have never heard anyone say it — that almost every Negro woman you see downtown among the shoppers and clerks and ranchers is young and is going into the hospital in a white uniform and is quite pretty: indeed, you reflect that they are probably all of a single family — the Campbells, or the Thompson Wheats — and they have a dignity and ease and poise that makes them seem like elegant Untouchables-in-white-stockings. . . . And of course you see, as you can see almost every day, the picture-taking man on his bicycle — Ace Starnes — as he moves gingerly among the cars in traffic, his long legs peddling evenly, his brown-bush moustache deeply tobacco stained, his jacket pockets bulging with flash bulbs and baby pictures and pints of Old Crow.   ⋛

— On the schoolground the afternoon is languid, floating on its own stillness.

The two o'clock air moves idly about, making a kind of nuzzling love to the shade of the oak trees and to the resting cement steps outside the high-school doors.

The March sun is out, providing light and a friendly warmth, but it does not intrude on the thin, cool air. It is saving itself for more heat-and-glare-ridden days.

Nothing really moves.

The school buildings themselves are resting. Classes have disappeared inside them as if into great stone morgues.

The shaded waterfountains and trimmed hedges are tending to their own affairs. Professional solitaries, they are used to amusing themselves quietly through the long stretches of impersonal afternoon. They wait, drowsing within metal and shining green leaves.

At the edge of the schoolground a clump of low shinoaks stand in shade, their bark looking smooth from a distance, almost sensual, like the skin of wet seals. They are frozen in a private oak-dance, trunks slanting here and there, but their heads are joined communally, in a modest, perpetual union. Their bodies go roundly, firmly, separately, into the young spring grass — like gun barrels into green velvet.　　　　　　　　　⮞

— Lovesickness eats at me while I take a sunbath on the wooden doors of the flower pit behind the house. I lie there on the quilt, hiding my thin white body from the street, thinking of Roberta Crowley driving around town in a college boy's blue station wagon.

I have a towel over my eyes; I can smell the sweat gathering in the crevices of my neck and armpits; red ants are crawling across the quilt. I have begun to smell strongly of skin and sun and sweat. From inside the house I can hear "Nature Boy," by Nat King Cole, on the record player.

I lie there, thinking of Roberta in the blue station wagon, and waiting for an ant to sting me.　　　　　　　　　　⮞

— *sheep: They meander along in the late afternoon, nose down in the tall needle grass. They walk so casually, so indifferently, that they do not seem to be moving at all, alive at all. They are like pasteboard cutouts on a slowly revolving, pastureland stage.*

Occasionally some abrupt sound disturbs the air and they

come to life. Heads raise and fail to chew for a moment, listening. Perhaps a hawk has called from the top of a post oak tree, or a Diesel truck has honked on a road across the valley. The sheep consider the noise, weigh it against the peace that follows, and finally decide that it represents no violation or threat. There is nothing new in the air that a sheep should get excited about. So, as one, they bend their necks down toward the grass again and eat — their marble eyes hidden behind bundles of needle spears, their bodies again lifeless as smooth rocks scattered here and there across the ground. ⋑

— Daddy puts kerosene under the pendulum of the grandfather clock to make it keep steady time. "It loosens up the joints," he says. He puts a jarlid full of kerosene inside the box where the pendulum is and after winding the clock up tight, he sets the pendulum swinging. He watches it for a long while to see that it doesn't stop and then shuts the glass door. Mother keeps saying that kerosene can't possibly do any good. But once, when the pendulum stopped, Daddy opened the little door and saw that the jarlid was empty. "See, now," he said, "that proves it." ⋑

— *on the ranchhouse porch:* Six-thirty, on a May afternoon, and Gram, my grandmother, has laid the front yard water hose in the canna bed and is now sitting in the green porch chair for a while before she goes inside to fix supper. Plump, gray-haired, wearing her faded apron and worn canvas shoes, she is as familiar to me as my own breathing.

I am seated nearby on the steps, looking south toward the distant blue hills near home. I am where the peace of the ranch seems to focus itself at sundown and I sit there, untroubled and content.

As I gaze out across the yard I know that all I have to do is turn around and I can look back through the house and out the screen of the dining room window to where the sun is still coming down hard on the garden, the rock water tank, the peach orchard. I am sitting there on the steps — with the steady south breeze coming into the partly shadowed, deep-green yard — but I can easily turn, if I want to, and see the sun-bathed bodies of flies swarming above the back walk, still vigorous, still afternoon-alive. . . .

The doves have begun to settle in the big oaks west of the house. I listen to them, and it is as if the air is being seduced by their soft dove noises. They are soothing the late afternoon the way they always do — caressing it with languid, melting calls. . . . And I can hear the sheep bleating far out in the pasture. Their bleats — mild, frantic, solitary — drift in like brief dying smoke signals of sheep-loneliness and sheep-hysteria.

Behind us, the rooms of the ranchhouse are quiet except for the steady rhythm of the mantel clock and the humming of the refrigerator. Then, flatly, the back door slams and Grandpa's boots come toward us like notes of familiar kitchen music: heavy, hesitant, clumping, sliding along. They go, heel first, across the kitchen floor and on toward the bathroom.

Gram and I continue to sit, not talking, looking out, waiting for Grandpa to join us on the porch as the afternoon sinks into itself all around us. ⋙

A Case of Survival

W LET ME TELL YOU ABOUT a young man and his search for love. It started early one fall when he decided to leave his home town and cast his spirit in a new place. During most of the year he had been involved with Charlotte, who loved him but for whom he could not summon up a similar love. And it was love, passionate love, that he wanted above all other things. He wanted to be shaving at seven o'clock in the morning and suddenly think of his girl and be immensely glad. At twenty-five he wanted ecstasy.

It had hurt them both, that long spring and summer, to watch for signs of his love, like anxious parents waiting for the birth of their first child. They had had companionship and an utter closeness, but ecstasy never appeared for the young man. Sometimes he had spoken to Charlotte with a hurtful honesty, as if to inoculate her against false hope and disillusion — or at least keep her love contained within her so it would not overflow. But her love had overflowed, and often; for long minutes after midnight he would hold her while she cried on their dark, familiar street.

To free his spirit, or perhaps even to test it, he left for the city that fall. At first he felt neither buoyant nor full of despair. He told himself that he and Charlotte would just have to wait and see. That was the sum of his wisdom at the moment, since all other attempts at wisdom had failed. But as he thought more deeply about his move he knew that he was disentangling himself from Charlotte to allow fate a chance to bring him love out of the mists.

He was that far gone, this romantic young man; he was that willing to abandon himself wholly to love. He wanted to languish in the thought of it; he wanted to turn with sweet, agonizing pain on the rack of his emotions. In effect, he wanted to get on with the long-delayed business of creating his heaven on earth.

So that fall when he met the charming young secretary with the broken nose, he was like a thirst-crazed man finally dragging himself to the edge of a clear mountain stream. They worked in the same office building and often rode the elevator together to the fourth floor. She was blond, with her hair in bangs across her forehead and braided into a flat bun in the back. She looked Germanic, but he wasn't sure. She didn't talk overmuch or smile overmuch — just the amount he would have her talk or smile while riding with four or five people in an elevator. And when she got out she walked with her knees bent slightly forward, giving her a strange kind of sliding poise. But mainly it was her broken nose that intrigued him.

During those first days, when their eyes met briefly in the elevator and then passed on, when he knew he had already made the decision to approach her and ask her for a date, the young man would think: Now, isn't this exactly the way I knew it would begin, in just such circumstances, with just such a person? Didn't I know that I was waiting to be attracted to someone strongly and urgently, someone possessing both physical charm and physical blemish — and with the blemish actually serving to enhance the charm, finally becoming the very thing you learn to love as much as the charm itself?

Then, as if the earth's gravity had fluctuated momentarily, his insides would suddenly fall and he knew that he was going to think about Charlotte. The young man would clench his jaws and begin to defend himself loudly in his mind: All right, I didn't want it to happen; I didn't want to hurt Charlotte. I tried to love her, but it didn't work. And you shouldn't have to *try* to love someone. It should come more easily than anything else in the world. I knew I ought to leave it up to my instincts. And this proves it.

The young man would watch the secretary in the elevator. He observed her short, fleshy but pleasantly molded legs leaving before him as the elevator stopped at the fourth floor. And each time as he walked down the hall to his office and watched her disappear into hers, he would announce to his heart rather defiantly: I have to test it — that much is clear. I must never carry around a secret lust if things should ever work out with Charlotte. And if I should ask this new person to go out with me, and within an hour or a day or a week she is able to blot out or even appreciably diminish the whole long history of Charlotte and me, I will have been right to allow it to happen.

That, rather generally, is how it was that the young man came to escort Eloise Beatty to the Pink Elephant Lounge one Friday afternoon around five. There had been some hesitation on her part — a few traces of doubt or disinterest that flickered across her eyes. But she allowed herself to be walked two blocks down the street from their office building to the comfortable dark of the cellar lounge.

At first, though he struck enough casual poses and danced to the jukebox music with apparent sureness and ease, there was little peace in his mind. Above the ragtags of conversation and laughter he could hear himself talking furiously with his conscience: It *is* a justifiable fling! It's the kind of enjoyment I've been waiting for. I certainly wasn't getting anywhere the other way.

But the longer the young man argued with himself, the more he could not help feeling like a rogue and a cheat — not before the eyes of the law or social custom or even his own conscience but before the sharp, deep image of Charlotte and himself, standing off in the dimness of the bar, watching.

It was almost with dogged fury that he continued to drink the beer and urge the talk. The girl was going to appeal to him, she was going to fascinate him, she was going to get all the pent-up urges to love out of him — by *damn!* The beer began to heat him and they danced more often. Yes, this was the way it ought to be — it was exciting to hold her close and dance so luxuriously . . .

yes, she was warm and had a kind of sensual, electric aliveness to her skin . . . yes, he could find himself lingering on her features as she talked . . . yes, he felt rising within him that eagerness he had been waiting for.

And as time wore on during the late afternoon the young man became more and more an emotion engineer keeping a close watch on his pressure gauge, waiting for the needle of his emotions to quiver closer and closer to the point marked Love.

When they came up from the cellar lounge, hand in hand, it was deep twilight, and buildings and people along the sidewalks seemed pleasantly distant and vague. It had rained a little, and the wet leaves in the gutters gave a romantic touch to the streets.

They drove over to Eloise Beatty's apartment for coffee. The young man walked around the living room, listening to Eloise's remarks called out from the kitchen and examining little statuettes on shelves. When Eloise came out of the kitchen with cups of coffee on a tray, he was waiting. He took the tray from her and set it down carefully on the dining table and turned back to face her. He kissed her hard and full and very long, with the even, unhurried motions of an ecclesiastic performing a ritual. There was almost a detached quality about him, as though his real passion had already been expended in the long anticipation of such a moment and he was now just following through.

Eloise slid away from him slowly and smiled and picked up the tray again. Together they went over to sit on the couch. Both drank their coffee with a melodramatic slowness.

There was not a lot more kissing; the first surges of emotion were over. Actually, the young man felt it best that he leave Eloise rather quickly, before the inevitable counter-emotions set in. He knew that the beer and the twilight would be slipping up on them fast, and that soon they would begin to feel a little off-balance and awkward and unreal.

As he stood with her in the doorway he let his eyes go over

Eloise a final time to fix the image — full and placid face, lips without lipstick now, one blond braid loose and down across her shoulder, a rather soft-eyed look. He kissed her at length one final time; then they let their hands trail apart and, smiling, she closed the door.

As he walked back to his car he realized that in a way the whole thing depressed him, being able to visualize a romance in its entirety before it even began. He could see it all: the round face of Eloise appearing before him suddenly the next morning; his not being able to eat, just thinking of her; phoning her; going out with her and trying the small, intimate Italian restaurants; the bond between them gradually growing stronger. . . .

And sooner or later he would have to write Charlotte.

No control over passions, no control over life — the thought slightly irked him. But he was too hungry and tired to anguish much over life right then. He sighed and rubbed his neck. Darkness had come, and had brought with it a cooling night breeze. The mild depression within him began to fade, and by the time he got close to his car he was almost bouncing along — not swaggering, but unusually jaunty. Yes, he thought, I guess by the time I'm an old geezer about eighty I will have tasted a few fruits in life. And I guess that's about all you can ask.

The young man opened the door of his car almost gently, as if he were mellowed and a little world-weary with insights. He decided he had better put aside — for the time being, at least — Eloise Beatty and her charmingly broken nose. She would be haunting him enough later on as it was; he might as well begin being haunted on a full stomach.

Yet it was not until he was eating breakfast in a drugstore the next morning that he suddenly remembered. Why, I should have been deep into my romance hours ago! he thought. Surely her golden braids and her quick little floating laugh haunted me during the night; surely when morning came I lay there in bed, languid and rapturous in the thought of her.

The young man ate a little of his grapefruit and tried to recall: What had been the first thing he thought of that morning? When he remembered, he put down his spoon and smiled; it was the habit Charlotte had of unconsciously swinging her long, tanned leg whenever she sat on the front-porch steps back home and got wound up telling something involved and ridiculous about her East Texas Baptist kinfolks. His smile lingered awhile, faltered, began to fade. For a moment he merely sat there, sobered by his recollection.

Then gradually, involuntarily, the young man's lips came apart — almost in awe, as they might have if he had been Moses receiving the tablets of stone from the hand of God — and he spoke out loud to the drugstore counter the words that were beginning to tumble around inside his head, words he still could not quite believe: "Charlotte . . . she survived; *Charlotte survived.*"

And leaving his raincoat, newspaper and plateful of uneaten eggs, the young man slid off his stool and ran across the street through the heavy eight-thirty traffic. He stood inside the glass telephone booth, nodding, gesturing, turning this way and that as the long-distance operator placed his call and a familiar buzzing began to come through the receiver.

What if she didn't answer, or even *refused* to? What if she wasn't at home? What if — Lord, think of it! — what if she had even got herself involved with somebody else? Impossible, of course. Not good old Charlotte. Not the one girl who could always be counted on, who always *understood.* Why didn't she answer? She was bound to be home this time of the morning. Unless . . .

And then — *yes,* there it was: her voice finally, sleepy-sounding, wonderfully familiar, a delicious pleasure to hear.

The young man slumped against the side of the phone booth, feeling weak and content, just barely able to enjoy the private little ecstasy of hearing the voice in the receiver say over and over again, "Hello? Hello? Who is this, please? Hello? . . ." ≷

Texas Journal

I : Clearing the Air

W SHE WORE STRAIGHTFORWARDNESS like a chastity belt: "There's one thing you must realize, Paul, before we go any further. I think it's only fair to both of us." Tap, tap, went her cigarette against the smooth spaghetti house table, almost seeming to nod its head in agreement. "I've always had people take me exactly for what I am, and I certainly don't intend to stop doing any differently tonight. I'm always honest with people I associate with and if it turns out that someone doesn't want to be honest with me — well, then, there's simply no point in us ever pursuing the thing any further."

I was seated directly across from them at another table. I could see her eyes snap dramatically behind black-rimmed glasses as she carefully spaced her next words.

"The best compliment I ever received — and it's something I will never forget, Paul; I value it that much — was when a boy I had been dating told me, 'Alma, I have respect for you, and I can't say that about most of the girls I go out with. You're a square-shooter; you're always willing to speak your mind.' And Paul, you know that we parted friends? But I had to lay my cards on the table first and tell him exactly — just as I have been telling you — *exactly* the kind of girl he was taking out. I had to set him straight, and because I did I believe he appreciated it more than ever later on."

I could not tell if Paul was appreciating much of anything. His big square back did not move.

"Now I believe that's the only way two people can get along; I sincerely mean it." Tap, tap. "And if you don't think I'm the kind of girl you want to take out for the rest of the evening now that I've cleared the air, so to speak, well then, Paul, we at least know where we stand, and I don't think there's anything more important in this world than that — no matter what you thought when you asked me out . . . I sincerely believe, from the things you've intimated, that I'm not at all what you had in mind when you called me up."

What Paul had in mind when he called her up was never quite clear. I'm not even sure what he had in mind when he carefully picked up his water glass and threw the water in Alma's face and walked out of the spaghetti house. But Alma did stop talking. And after the waiter brought a towel she even finished her lasagna. ⋙

II : *Betty Lee*

W EACH FALL AFTERNOON she changed from her starched school dress to clean blue jeans and a flannel shirt and went outside to do the chores. She gathered eggs from the barn, watered the rabbits in their cages beside the garage, scattered corn in the woodlot for the guineas — and all the while kept whistling and scuffing her shoes and listening to my uncle call "gooooatie, gooooatie, gooooatie" down below the hill in the creek pasture.

I remember her best that way — growing up so easily at her ranch home among chickens and horses and cedar trees. She was my cousin Betty Lee: a pretty, soft-faced girl with brown hair and a small childish voice who liked to sit at dusk on the back porch and shell pecans while my uncle chopped wood for the fireplace. She was always happy in these long early years — did not once realize that life could ever be more than raising fawns and baking fudge and sewing dressing for the FHA.

Then, out of the blue, things happened to Betty Lee: she got married, moved away, had a baby, became sick. It all seemed too much, too sudden — at seventeen she knew nothing about Los Angeles or husbands or polio. She knew quite a bit less about iron lungs and dying. She was simply not prepared.

I kept asking myself afterwards: What would you have her do — stay out there forever along that cedar ridge, whistling "Red Wing" and trailing corn to the guineas? Would you keep her permanently thirteen, prevent her from meeting her fate?

No, I would say . . . but I still find it hard to drive to her house any more. In my mind it has always stayed November along the Harper Road, and Betty Lee is always there in her blue jeans and plaid shirt — calling out in her clear, innocent, childish voice to the animals, the ranch, the world, to me.

III : *Beer*

AFTER A PERSON GROWS UP he rarely takes time even to smell — much less ponder — a bottle of beer. For the adult, beer simply becomes a matter of opening up and drinking down. The taste and the heightening effect is what counts.

But I can remember the days when the closest I got to beer was the smell.

It was when Grandpa used to stop at a drive-in on his way back to the ranch and order himself a Falstaff or two while Gram and I had our Delaware Punch. I would only get a whiff from the top of the bottle before he poured the beer into a glass, but that smell was a beautiful thing to consider: rich and dry and clean, it cut across our overly sweet Delawares like an aroma from an underground garden — some secret place where small vegetations breathed in a chilled silence.

And as I remember it, even the bottles appeared more symbolic, more magical then. A darker duller brown, sitting rather austere and phallic on Grandpa's window tray, they seemed like another set of quiet spokesmen for that strange adult world which, though always surrounding me, was something constantly ahead, something perpetually and illusively *beyond*. They remained there for years on the horizon of Grandpa's car: dark obelisks luring me out of childhood.

IV : *Sunday Women*

IF YOU HAPPEN to be outside your house some Sunday after church, listen to the sound of the women inside as they move around getting the table ready for dinner. Listen, and hear rising from the house a kind of song: the Song of Womankind. It is a simple tune, nothing more than the melody of high-heeled shoes echoing and re-echoing across the wooden dining room floor. . . .

Yet these long solos of stabbing heels show not just woman's Sunday talent but her genius as well — that special and curious power which is never duplicated by the genius of any man. For only a woman can wear such heels and make such sounds — awkward and clattering, yet somehow precise and imperious too; only a woman can produce such hollow, quick-stepping noises that not only balance but actually surmount the short-comings she may have found herself involved in during the other six days of the week. It is as though the women are saying through the Song: "Look, within the past brief hour we have managed to recoup our loses and are once again what our men thought they were marrying in the first place: something utterly feminine and utterly unique, something so profoundly different from themselves that they know they must have us regardless of any penalty or price."

And those heels, just by crossing and recrossing the dining room floor, just by their hurried rhythmic code, are able to bring to you, the listener, the whole magic and lure and image of Sunday Woman: her powder-and-perfume smell, the sliding of her hosed legs and thighs against each other, her firm and intimate brassiere, her newly penciled eyebrows, the ornaments for her ears and hair and fingers and dress, the lure of her softer flesh. . . . Those heels, echoing past the gently waving curtains of the dining room windows — they sing the bright Sunday message of rebirth as only a woman can compose it: with a sort of brisk off-handed accuracy that so surprises and enlists the male listener that he is left without the necessity or even the desire for comment.

And if, indeed, you are there, outside the house, then listen later *beyond* the heels, to the chorus of woman-talk coming from the kitchen. Listen to that jungle of sounds out of which, from time to time, the long shrieks of woman-laughter rise like the shrill crying of birds or monkeys — with quickly grown supporting laughter racing along in its wake like a scattering of more monkeys or more birds. Then hear the way in which the violent disturbance soon passes — how the laughter returns to the tree-tops of the kitchen again, how the talk settles and balances until the jungle is sober again.

. . . You can almost visualize the women as they stand grouped around dishes of food on the tables and stove; you can almost follow the many separate pairs of hands that are busy slicing lemons and tomatoes and avocadoes into waiting dishes while similarly isolated and autonomous mouths lock themselves into great, easy, comfortable smiles — smiles spread to full, Sunday-dinner preparation width. And if you try, before you walk around the corner of the house and come back inside, you can almost see their brains too. They are equally autonomous, and instead of guiding and controlling the hands and mouths they are merely other separate body parts existing in a kind of Sunday neutral gear — pleasantly idling, pleasantly unurging and unurged, sufficient within themselves: women's brains. **⋑**

v : *Lucia*

Ꞷ LUCIA JOHNSON was a Negro girl, aged 13, who sat to the right of my desk as I faced my eighth grade reading class. After the first few weeks of school I never looked to see if she had brought her library book: I knew it would be there in her lap, ready to be opened at the marker when there was a lull in the class or when she had finished her work for the day.

She was very quiet, very neat in her work and in the way she dressed. Her black hair was always carefully pulled into a mixture of smoothness and braids, and she usually wore a kind of pony tail in back. Her body was small and almost fragile; her skin was a smooth and very light brown; her features were clean and delicate. She always looked as though her mother had just finished dressing her for Sunday school — as if she had just got through standing very still while her mother helped her into her starched dress and tied the ribbon across her hair and laid out the white socks and rubbed the black leather shoes to a high gleaming shine.

Sometimes when I looked at her face, at the large eyes and the finely chiseled nose and mouth and cheek bones, I thought I was looking secretely at a small, contented deer: a fawn momentarily at peace because there were no hunters around to bother it: a fawn still able, however, from a deep instinct, to keep the nerves sensitive and the expression alert.

Whenever it was Lucia's turn to read aloud in class, it was like being sick and having a nurse put cool towels on your forehead and gently re-arrange your pillows. Her voice was throaty and careful and unhurried, a pleasant balm for your ears. She seldom mispronounced a word, but if she did she stopped and waited for me to pronounce it for her; then she pronounced it exactly as I did and went on, still just as careful and obedient to the lines on the page as before, still like the father of a family who is a good driver and turns the curves of a high mountain road at just the right speed to suit his wife. And if the class had not been listening very closely to other readers, they suddenly began to follow the words when Lucia read them. For there was a dignity that showed in her voice, and a proper concern for her duty as a reader. It was not a voice of high seriousness or dramatic power; it was simply Lucia Johnson, reading — talking to us all with a clear, firm yet soft and Southern Negro voice.

I liked to watch Lucia as she went down the hallway to her classes. She never walked too fast or too slow, but always moved in a way that indicated she had a definite place to go and a definite time to be there. If I had ever tried to draw her motion with a pencil, I would have done it the way a child draws the ocean's surface, with many slight dips — all the same size, and all connected. She walked steadily, one hand down beside her, holding her clarinet case, and the other hand across her breast, holding in her books. She never slouched along, as though resisting where she was going; nor did she ever seem to be late.

Lucia, by just being Lucia, was always fine enough. But whenever she would break into a slow smile and give one of her throaty, flat laughs — that was when she slipped charm into the day. I remember one afternoon when I was almost late for a one o'clock class and was striding fiercely down the hall toward my room. I don't know exactly why but just as I got to the door I turned around, and there was Lucia and her friend Henrietta, stalking side by side behind me with the longest steps they could muster. Both were smiling, Henrietta widely and with a great display of white in her dark round face, and Lucia eagerly but still shyly, with a kind of private amusement. She said, "Sir, Henrietta and Ah have been *followin* you." Had anyone else said that, I probably would have given a professional smile in acknowledgement and hurried on. But to turn around and find Lucia there, her small deer-slim legs almost wobbling across the floor in their hurry, to think about her sharing smiles with Henrietta and enjoying their secret alliance all the way down the hall — to simply consider Lucia and her moment of gentle fun as she mocked the teacher and his long legs — it was like reaching out and smoothing down the hair of someone you love. It was just that simple, and that nice.   ⋙

VI : *Knowing*

Ⓦ OUT AT THE LOTS a lamb bleats. He doesn't know that Grandpa is dead.

I am walking out there underneath the tin roof, looking in at quiet dark rooms and sheds, and I come upon him.

"Baaa." He bleats and jams himself toward me from within his pen.

"Grandpa is dead," I say to him. "Did you know that? Can't you just feel the difference?"

"Baaa. . . ."

He thinks I will feed him. He has his head through an opening in the boards. I stoop and rub his nose and he tries to grab hold of my thumb to suck. I look at him and then cup my hand over his round knobby head. It's a good feeling. It has been a long time since I felt the pleasant way a lamb's head feels.

"Baaa."

I walk on and leave him in his innocence. And it's all right. He doesn't have to know about things. My knowing — that's enough.   ⋟

VII : *A Small, Mild Man*

ᗑ HE WAS SITTING in a Denton cafe booth with two brown-suited pals, having coffee. At first I thought all three were from the big Baptist church across the street — I had forgotten about the nearby funeral home.

It was a warm April afternoon, and the men were leaning back a little from the coffee cups, idling through their small talk. The two men in brown suits were discussing their teen-aged children — how much they ate, how fast they were growing. One of them said he had measured his sixteen-year-old boy just the other night: had stood him straight and square-shouldered in the bedroom while making a higher pencil mark on the bedroom door.

The small mild man, who had been mainly listening until now, tapped his cigarette against his coffee saucer and said, rather brightly, "Well, when I measure 'em, they're dead."   ⋟

VIII : *In San Elizario*

ᗑ I STOOD IN THE DOORWAY of an old abandoned building, east of El Paso, gazing out into the fading summer afternoon. The shadow of the building had finally begun to jut into the small

clearing out front, making a smooth layer of suggestiveness over tranquil, five o'clock dirt. I stood there, watching a colony of bees swarming in the pale sunlight — and behind them, in a ditch, a red-winged blackbird that rode contentedly on the top of a thick, swaying reed.

To the left of the clearing the San Elizario Catholic Church was resting in its own quiet splendor, its white sides gleaming in the sun. From time to time pigeons would wheel suddenly from its roof and head purposefully, almost violently, into the sky — as if carrying urgent dispatches to the moon.

As I kept looking about, watching the day end, I noticed a row of telephone poles crossing a cotton field. *Telephone poles:* how long, I wondered, had it been since I had really looked at them? . . . I considered them a moment, in their neatness and symmetry, and decided that they were still in pretty good shape; that they had managed, over the years, to retain a wholesome telephone-pole integrity. I wanted to salute them in my mind as stoic partners of the land.

After a while the west wind began to rise. It moved along, stirring the cottonwood leaves, touching the grass, until finally the afternoon seemed ready to contemplate itself again in another long private moment before dark. I heard dogs barking in the distance; crickets began to make their first tentative noises from the ditch. . . . Yes, I thought, deeper moods are possible now: over there, beyond the church, that white school building is becoming intimately involved with elm tree shade. . . . And — Jesus God, it is almost too much: there is the smell of wood smoke, and the sound of a piper cub humming along the horizon. . . .

As I stood there, sunk in peace, I had the overpowering urge to *do* something about the scene before me — to transfix it, somehow, so it would not be lost; to take the mood of the silent mountains and the whistle of dove wings and give them their proper immortality. Yet it was like all the other times when the essence of life seemed to be rising like vapor out of the ground and I was almost physically hurting with the pain of knowing that such good moments were dying unheralded, uncelebrated: I watched and felt and accepted the truth: that no one could perpetuate bliss.

So, until dark, I remained in the doorway of the crumbling adobe house — bathed by the cooling air, mildly cheered by bees, feasting on the sadness and the elegance of the quietly living earth. ⟾

In the Bus Station

1 : *Shoeshine*

W "LET'S SHINE 'EM UP, NOW. Hey, how 'bout it? *Nice* little shine. . . ."

He was in his forties, maybe fifties, this Negro shoe shine man in the El Paso bus station. He had on his Gauguin shirt — a red, short-sleeved one with big splotches of blue and green flowers — and lumberjack boots. He barely looked up from his customer's shoe to call out the chant to the passersby.

A young soldier in starched khakis came out of the bus station cafe and the shoe shine man sang out to him: "All *ri-ight;* you're nex'." The call had a touch of authoritative briskness that made it seem like a command: it was a bit of shrewdness by the Negro, playing on the reflexes of the unsure recruit. The soldier paused, looked first at the Negro and then down at his shoes. He stood there, undecided, until the Negro — without missing a stroke of his polishing rag — gave a stern beckoning nod toward the unoccupied chair just above his head. "Sure, now," he said, "you need it. Have a seat ri'chere nex' this gentleman and fix you up in a jiffy."

The shoe shine man kept on working rhythmically, doggedly, the smoke from his bouncing cigarette curling around the tip of the customer's shoe. The soldier in the door — just killing time, anyway, until the next bus — decided Ah, Well, What The Hell. He walked toward the shine stand with swaggering slowness: any faster movement might show that he was not his own boss, that the Negro had truly intimidated him into a shine. He hunched his shoulders forward a little and then just before climbing into the empty seat he gave one last critical glance down at his shoes — as if to satisfy himself that they really could stand a little touching up, after all. The Negro ignored him, kept calling out, "Ri'chere . . . nice little shine. . . ." ➣

II : *The Slowly Walking Fellow*

TALL AND THIN, the seat of his dirty khaki pants black with tar, he circled the waiting room of the bus station. He walked slowly, as if carefully tracing the edge of sanity.

After making a half dozen tours the man sat down on a bench — sat with the same tense control he used in walking. He crossed his long legs, placed a cigarette in his mouth, then searched for a match with his strange purplish hands. There was no hair on them or on his wrists; they were completely smooth — as if the hair had been slicked off by months of riding freight trains in sub-zero weather. His fingernails had lost their moons and were swollen, rounded, almost pendulous: Ubangi-lip nails. They were like curious plants that would soon grow to bursting-size and drop little rosy-colored, round, moonless discs.

The man stared down at his army surplus shoes, silently moving his lips. The muscles in his jaws were like hidden panels sliding around beneath his skin, trying to create sound. The face was bony and inward and haunted, yet it seemed to have been charged once with great intelligence: the face of a J. Robert Oppenheimer after the Bataan death march.

With almost boyish gracefulness, the man finally rose from the bench, walked across to where two young soldiers were talking, and asked if they had a dime for a cup of coffee. He spoke with a surprisingly deep, quiet voice, and for a moment it was as if you were listening to an afternoon radio program during the early 1940's: Dr. Anthony Phillips saying in well-modulated tones, "Miss Gaylord, could I see the Simmons chart, please."

The man took the dime and resumed his slow circling of the waiting room — the high-domed, skull-like head looking awkward with its skidrow haircut, the purple hands and wrists dangling far out of the wrinkled coat, the lips searching constantly for meaning. He kept moving at a steady, thoughtful pace, touching each foot to the floor lightly. His footsteps gave no sound. ⋞

III : *No Scales in Pomona*

W A GRAYING MEXICAN MAN sat on the waiting room bench, rubbing his knee. A young college boy sat in the seat next to him.

"It's better to have girls," he advised the boy. "They don't give you so much trouble." He was disillusioned about his two grown sons, who still kept saying 'How about twenty dollars, papa?' even after they had their own families. He touched the college boy very lightly on the leg and told him he would not regret it, having girls. "If you say to them, 'Stay home,' they will cry in their room — but they will stay there. And later everything will be all right; they do not hold grudges. But boys — they will say they are just going to the grocery store, and when they get outside, *poof* — off they go."

He said he gave his mother, who was 83 and lived in Sweetwater, a little money every month; usually it was just a dollar out of his social security check. But his brothers did not give her anything. He had seen one of his brothers make as much as $700 in a single day and not think of his mother once. He said that he had asked his brother, who owned a wrecking yard, 'Why don't you give mama something? Today you made $700.' And the brother had said, 'Well, I have a lot of things to take care of.'"

The Mexican man shook his head. "Your mama borns you and helps you when you are little — wipes you, keeps you going — and then when you make $700 you cannot give her something."

He talked on for a while, telling the college boy that he was on his way back to Sweetwater from Pomona, California, where one of his daughters lived. He was going to stay by himself at his little house in Sweetwater and eat Post Toasties. "I am too fat," he said. He pulled a little brown bottle from the pocket of his khaki shirt and wiggled it in the air. In Pomona, he said, he only had to take two of the pills for his heart. The climate was

good for him; also, he didn't eat very much. He said that one day he only had Post Toasties for breakfast, nothing else all day, and he felt so good that he wanted to run down the street. He had walked around in front of his daughter's house and his wife told him that he was going to have a spell for sure. "I told her, no, I just did not eat nothing today and it was all right around my heart." So his wife was staying there in Pomona while he took the bus back home and lost some more weight.

"How old do you think I am?" he asked the boy suddenly, taking off his hat. His hair was gray. "I asked an Indian man in Phoenix how old he thought I was; I bet him ten dollars he could not guess my age. The Indian man said, 'No, I won't take your money because I can tell exactly how old you are. You are 57, or several months on either side.' And do you know that Indian man sure would've got my money. I am 58, but I think I look 78 because my hair is almost all white. Well, it was my heart that did it. And my left eye is out. . . ."

The loudspeaker finally called his bus, and he began to adjust his hat. He patted the college boy on the shoulder and told him again it was better to have only girls. "You know, whenever I get ready to die — when I am very sure — I am going to tell my two daughters but not my two sons. They would just say, 'Papa, let me have twenty dollars'— and me on my way into the ground."

He stood up, holding his paper sack of belongings. "And you want to know something else? They don't have any scales in Pomona. The day I ate just Post Tosties I wanted to weigh myself, and I couldn't find a place to do it. When I write my daughter I am going to tell her, 'cause that is the only thing I don't like about that place." ⧓

IV : *Off to Vietnam*

W THE GEORGIA SOLDIER sat in the bus station cafe, softly singing the words to a Webb Pierce record as it played on the jukebox. He was seated across from his big-boned Georgia wife, who was wearing a red and yellow hippie costume. Holding her elbows in his cracked, plowboy hands, he gazed into her face and sang.

The soldier's daughter sat in the seat beside him, eating ice cream. She had the pale, thin, unsmiling face of a European refugee, and large blue eyes, and while the soldier sang she looked carefully at the people passing by.

The mother did not wear any lipstick and had on white make-up that caked her face like a geisha mask. Her hair was dyed a crow's wing black. When she smiled she showed very large, even teeth.

The soldier was concerned about his daughter's health. He kept asking the girl to open her mouth and say Ah, and as he looked into her throat he said, "Mama, them tonsils sure look bad." His wife did not seem to hear. She gazed vaguely away from the table, smiling to herself, humming.

The soldier was in uniform and wore short khaki sleeves. He had sandy, curly hair on his forearms and there were freckles on his face like splotched shoe polish. He was just another Good Old Country Boy, headed to Vietnam — leaving Mama to look after his thin, pale-faced daughter.

They sat, played the juke box, drank from their water glasses until it was time for the soldier's bus. As the soldier got up from the table he put his arm around his wife and smiled at her a little. She picked carefully at a scab on her finger and hummed a Bob Dylan tune.

v : *A Man*

NINE O'CLOCK AT NIGHT and a man was seated on a bench, leaning over on his knees. He was drunk, tired, worn out, and he was also very sick. The flu, perhaps. From time to time he dropped his head and coughed between his knees in a weak, soft way.

He seemed quite alone in the world. Perhaps he wanted to get back to Los Angeles — mother city of the West for castoffs, strays — but was out of money. Perhaps he was stranded in El Paso on the bus station bench.

. . . You looked at the man and tried to imagine him as he once might have been: strong and capable. You thought of him back in his home town during the 1940's: a strapping Robert Stack of a fellow in his blue and gold football uniform: smiling, the helmet held casually underneath his arm, the dark hair curled with afternoon sweat, his sunken blue eyes steady and direct and full of the knowledge that he was not just handsome and tough but also exceptionally shrewd in getting what he wanted from people. And then you imagined him a bit later, after a hitch in the navy, say: back home again, still aggressive and dashing but his eyes not quite as direct: for he had a family now — two kids and a blond-haired, thin-mouthed wife — and he was getting a reputation as a drinker. He was still reliable, though: was still a steady worker during the day on his bread truck route. . . .

The man on the bench rallied a bit, coughed, managed to bring up his head. He reached unsteadily toward his pants pocket, struggled in it a moment, found his dirty gray wad of a handkerchief. He feebly tried to blow his nose into it; missed; tried again; missed; continued to blow past it into his fingers.

For a while the man sat straightened up, working hard to keep his eyes from closing. He batted them slowly, above the great sagging pouches of wrinkled skin, and they were like fish mouths gulping for air. The red eyelids strained, the eyeballs rolled.

He searched and found a cigarette in his right front pocket, then held it in his fingers for a while as he tried to master himself

— tried to gear his body to meet the challenge of finding a match. After wobbling his head for a bit, and blinking, he managed to turn a little toward the man sitting in the row of benches behind him. He opened his mouth, hoped he was saying it—Hey, buddy, you got a light? — but the words blurred and faded and the man behind him went on reading. The sick man lost control of his neck muscles and his head swung back. His eyes closed again, his chin sank to his chest.

The man sat that way, bent over, beaten.

And so worn out. That was what struck you most about him. His virility gone. His spirit leaked away. The stench from his body like a wolf's breath. . . . You looked at the jacket stained with vomit, the wrinkled black pants caked with mud. You looked at the creases in his neck and face: they were like the deep slashes of a turtle's mouth. This man — you thought it in a kind of wonder and disbelief: this man was destroyed; at forty-five he had blown himself out. It was as though time had moved across his body like a strong electric current, and had crumpled him.

Suddenly the man stirred and got awkwardly to his feet. He balanced himself for a moment, then began to stagger toward the baggage counter. He just got a step or two before he lurched into the metal trash container at the end of the aisle. He knocked it to the floor with a loud clatter, and sprawled across it. As the passengers from the 9:15 bus began to enter the waiting room the man lay there among the scattered paper and orange peels — Robert Stack just short of the goal line, his eyes gulping, his unlit cigarette still jutting from between his fingers.   ⋛

VI : *Ab Snopes*

ᗯ IT WAS NOT his mild growth of beard that was remarkable; it was his eyes — unblinking beneath their pale, almost non-existent eyebrows. They were like the small almond eyes of a

Mongol, gazing out at the world through the face of Garth the Swineherd.

The man was standing beside the row of telephone booths, quietly chewing, wearing a small dark hat and black motorcycle boots. He looked rather trim and spare in his clothes, yet he did not actually seem to be wearing them: he did not give the impression that he got up each morning and routinely put on his shirt, jacket, jeans. It was more as if he lived in them — as if they had grown to him, gradually, like a second skin.

The man stayed in the waiting room an hour or so, moving about only to watch and chew. Once he stood in back of a boy playing a pinball machine. With his hands in his pockets he watched the boy beat rhythmically against the wooden rim and listened to the heavy clicks of the machine. The boy turned around, to see who had come up behind him, but the man did not shift his gaze — did not give the slightest indication that either he or the boy was standing there. He just moved his jaws steadily and gazed past the boy's shoulder into the flashing lights.

The man never changed expression. One could not have told if he were watching a couple fornicating, or goldfish swimming in a bowl, or a volcano beginning to erupt. He did not register emotion. It was as though he had stepped bloodlessly and directly — a pure word creation — out of a Faulkner novel: had come to El Paso to see for himself just how different things were out West from Old Miss'sip.

Only once did the man seem on the verge of thought. His jaws continued to work the tobacco gently and his narrow eyes still looked out direct and unblinking, but he seemed almost ready to say to himself, unimpressed: "Sho, now . . . just folks sitting around on benches, same as any place. God-damn." He stood a while longer beside the photo booth, then seemed to disappear. Perhaps he simply caught a bus, or drifted on out into the street. Perhaps he went to look at another bus station. Or maybe he just eased on back into the mind of William Faulkner, where he could be more comfortable.　　　　$\gtrless$

VII : *Not Many Flars on the Grave*

☿ A HUGE WHITE-HAIRED WOMAN was telling a very thin, broken-down man about the death of her husband. The two of them were seated on a bench, turned in slightly toward each other. The woman wore a print cotton dress, the man a wrinkled sports coat and gray work pants. They both spoke with a country twang, but the man's was stronger.

"He jest carried me on a silver platter," the fat woman was saying. "He worshipped me, the very ground I walked on."

The man was nodding steadily; he could see it, the grandness of her marriage, its flowering. He kept his mouth open, as though his jaws were wired or his adenoids had gone bad. He sat with his bony legs crossed, with one arm propped on his knee so that the smoke from his cigarette coiled almost directly into the fat woman's face. But she didn't seem to mind; she was obviously lost to the golden days when she was on a platter.

Sitting there, sharing the woman's mood, the man began to ponder funerals. "Man-n-n-n-n," he said, "I don't believe in a-disturbin the day-ad." He said he was a soldier in that War Number Two and had gone in at that Normandy Beach. "Let me give it to ye straight, lady, I *knowed* it was gonna be rough when they told us, 'Now you kin all send a war home to your folks before you go across that channel.' So that's just what I done. I sent a war home to my good old mother in Pine Bluff and I said, 'Listen, maw, if anything a-happens to me that I don't get back, jest *leave me be*. . . . Yessir. . . . Why, man-n-n-n-n, it's that *second* funeral that's bad."

He took a drag from his cigarette and stared past the fat woman to the baggage counter, as if trying to get all his thoughts lined up about funerals and Arkansas and Normandy Beach. Apparently he got to thinking about cemeteries, too, for when he looked back to the fat woman he declared that times had changed: that nobody had respect for a buried man anymore. "Why," he said, "there's *freeways* on top of 'em."

The fat woman shook her head slowly and agreed that times were bad. She said that the way the world was headed, it wasn't going to be long before the Day of Reckoning. People dying, wars, drinking. . . .

She began to think of a friend of hers up near Alamogordo. "We was buddies," she said, holding her purse a little tighter against the great mound of her stomach. "He'd come to my ranch and I'd go over to his. We'd spend a couple of days that way . . . *you* know."

"Shore," the thin man said, nodding, seeing it.

"But he drank hisself to death. The doctor and me warned him. We said, 'You're goin to drink yourself to death.' But he was goin strong and he wouldn't listen. I was stayin up to his place for a while, you know. Well, finally I had to get back home and see about my chickens and things; and when I done up my chores and started back up that hill, I knowed somethin was wrong. And I went inside the door and he was cold dead."

"Shore," the thin man said. "Idn't that awful? But listen . . . I know about that 'cause I lost my very own mother — you'd know it was cancer without me even tellin — and you want to know what? I dug my own good mother's grave. Yessir. It was Christmas Day . . . in '47."

"That's supposed to be the day that Jesus Christ died, ain't it?"

The man was staring past her again, not listening. "Jest *shovel* it up and *spade* it in, *shovel* it up and *spade* it in. Man-n-n-n-n, I'm a hillbilly, but I'll tell you the truth: that jest cooked me to the bone."

"You got to know how to handle things," the fat woman said.

"I knowed a man once that left his family — all of them just stair-step childern — and went off with a woman. And now them childern is grown, and there's not a one of 'em that would step across the street to pull him out of a bar — "

"Man-n-n-n-n, idn't that what I been a-tellin ye: the goose hangs high."

"— and that man is this very day blind and just on one leg. . . . But let me tell you I ain't goin to be treated like that because I handled it right. I put my kids in church from the start. I prayed to the Lord and I said, 'Now listen, Lord,' and I talked to Him straight, just like I'm talkin to you. And ever one of my childern turned out good. . . . Why, I got a daughter in Fort Stockton, where I just been, and the way she treats me I'm a queen."

"You know, lady," the thin man said, "we ain't long for this-here earth, none of us, and that's a fact. But ever time I get to thinkin about things, like we jest been doin, I always remember about an uncle I onct had, a drinker. He didn't have no kids or nothin, and he was kinda mean. And I remember my maw a-sayin to us kids: She said, 'Your Uncle Oren don't know it but he's headed down a mighty lonesome road. He ain't gonna have many folks to miss him when he's gone'. . . . And little lady, she shore was right. They was jest 'leven people at his grave, and not many flars."

Saying that, the man leaned down a little on his crossed knees, almost dreamily, his cigarette smoke curling up past his long unshaven jaw and watery eyes. The fat woman continued to sit very straight with her hands over her purse. They did not face each other and both grew quiet — as though looking ahead, counting the flowers on their own lonesome graves. ❧

At the Border

I: *Contentment, and Milky Ways*

W THE MEXICAN MAN and his wife were in no hurry. They stopped beside the alligator pond in the plaza and looked a while. Most people do that — stare at the alligator as he lies submerged in the water with his snout breaking the surface or sunning on the gravel bank. People just like to contemplate the strangeness of such a creature. They hoist children to their shoulders in order for them to see better; they make many smiling comments to one another. The alligator seems to flavor the routines of their days.

The Mexican man stood with one work-toughened hand resting lightly on the top of the circular wall, not really looking in but instead just satisfied with being where people had gathered. The alligator could easily have been an atomic bomb or Orson Welles or Excalibur — it would have been pretty much the same. Phenomena did not really impress him (an alligator — what can you do with it? You cannot eat it; it does not provide you with cigarettes; there is no paycheck stuck to its tail. . . .) Yet he was willing to go along with these things the world set so much store by. After all, he was only an ignorant man, a laborer.

He wore cement-splotched shoes — big flat brogans — and had on a new straw hat and was clean shaven except for his moustache. He had a big, stolid, Indian's mouth, full and well-defined. He was rather tall for a Mexican — broad-shouldered, but also a little stooped. With his big feet he was a little too shambling and slow-moving to be the imposing figure of a man he might have been. Instead of being a moviestar leader of revolutions he seemed to be precisely what he was, a reliable bricklayer.

His wife, rather small and quite pregnant, stood beside him at the alligator pond like a loyal little pigeon. Her hair was pulled back tightly across her head and it hung behind her in a single black braid. She was not pretty and she wore no makeup, but her features were regular and clean in their plainness. She had a nice face to look at.

After a bit they walked together to one of the benches across the way and sat down. They continued to look at the strollers and the plaza and the streets and buildings beyond. The woman talked — never directly to her husband, just steadily and quietly to the air in front of them. The Mexican man sat forward a little, his elbows on his thighs and his big hands clasped between his legs. He looked straight ahead, occasionally indicating agreement with his wife by slight nods.

After sitting there a while the man reached into his pocket and pulled out two Milky Way candy bars. He partly unwrapped each bar — slowly, carefully, with a kind of genuine respect for the crinkling, injured sound of the paper — and handed one of them to his wife. She took it, and together they ate — the woman somewhat unnoticeably, continuing to talk; the man with a great flexing of his jaw and temple muscles that raised his straw hat a little with each chew. It took them a long time to finish — as though the candy bar were their dinner and they were making it last for a full lunch hour. Finally, when both were through, the man took the wrapper from his wife and they rose from the bench. They left the plaza as slowly as they had entered — the woman walking in front, the man slightly behind. Just before reaching the sidewalk the man stepped across to a bright green trash barrel and placed his wrappers inside. His wife waited at the sidewalk, and after he joined her, they both moved on. ⋟

II : *Crying Man*

𝖂 HE SAT CRYING BESIDE ME in a Juarez bar — not at all a person to be proud of, not someone whose tears and red eyes and running nose reflected a noble despair. He was just a young drunk Mexican who needed someone to tell his troubles to.

His home was in Los Angeles, where he had been arrested for drunken driving and had his license suspended. He still owed a big fine — something like $400 — and was supposed to go to jail for a couple of months. He had jumped bail, come to Juarez, lost whatever money he brought with him in two days and nights of drinking and being systematically robbed by prostitutes. And now he was telling me all this at three in the afternoon to convince me of the sorrowfulness of his plight.

From the moment he sat down next to me I wanted to leave. I did not want to be there on the barstool as he tried to keep the clear mucus wiped from his nose and poked me in the leg with his weaving forefinger. I did not want to look at the thick-coated edges of his dirty teeth whenever his mouth spread open in its twisted cry. I did not want to be frozen into vague, noncommittal stares toward my bottle of Carta Blanca and make equally vague and noncommittal noises as he sought to have me rage with him against the injustices of the world — especially the world that discriminated against him because he was a Mexican.

He soon pointed at a narrow red welt on his wrist, wanting me to examine it closely. I didn't know what it was — perhaps a small knife scar or maybe even some kind of infectious lesion. He pointed at it unsteadily with his other hand. "Handcuffs," he said. And as he smeared again at his nose with a perfunctory swipe of his arm he told me how he kept pleading over and over with the policemen, "It's too *tight,* too *tight,*" and how they hit him and rode around taking care of other business for an hour or so before finally taking him to the police station.

He kept looking at me intently, searching my face the way a drunk man will. How desperately he wanted me to minimize — even forget — his drunken driving and corroborate his feelings of injustice and rage; how he wanted me to jump off my stool and put my arm around his shoulder and say, Why, them dirty bastards! They didn't do all that to you, did they? Them bastards . . . let's me and you go get 'em — let's show 'em they can't push a guy around just because he's a Mexican (for wasn't I in a Mexican bar in Mexican Juarez? I couldn't be like those cops in L.A. who did all those wrong things against him — him with a wife and six kids; him with no money left and not able to drive a car any more and having to go to jail. And most important, him a good guy, a guy with no chance at justice anywhere. . . .)

I knew that, at the moment, I was probably the only person the crying man could talk to. No one else wanted to fool with him. I had seen the bartender walk away from him with that see-nothing, hear-nothing blandness that Mexican bartenders excel in and continue a game of cards with a fat, loud prostitute at the end of the bar. Two other prostitutes, slim shapely ones, the ones he had evidently spent all his money on, heard his pleadings and moanings for a little while and then shrugged and went upstairs to their rooms — leaving him standing in the middle of the bar with his arms outstretched, beginning to cry.

I kept thinking: what do you do with a drunk man you don't really care about — someone you don't like, much less respect; someone who is exploited by his own people until he is of no more use to them and is then ignored. Why should I bother to take any more of his blubberings and wailings. Whoever said I was my brother's keeper — especially when my brother turns out to be so distasteful.

And then my own reply hung itself before me in the air: My God, who do you show mercy to — good guys? Who are always the most in need of love — the lovable?

I didn't feel particularly good about it — I even felt that somehow I was doing wrong — but I continued to sit there on my stool. I didn't put my hand on the crying man's shoulder, buddy-like, and say that I enjoyed talking to him but had to run. I ordered another Carta Blanca and settled back to a second course of nose-wiping and disjointed raves. ঽ

III : *Jodl, of the Blighted Area*

ᘺ JODL ISN'T MARRIED, has no folks closer than Idaho. He is just a floater — a tall, fierce-browed man who piddles at some token job during the day and roams the downtown streets at night. He's older than I am — I would say about forty-two or -three — and from what I gather he has been drawing government disability checks since World War II. Though he has never come right out and said what happened — and have never felt myself enough of an intimate to ask — I have always assumed there is something wrong with his spine. He has a little rearing-back mannerism when he walks, and he gets up from cafe counters with a rather careful erectness. But nothing is really too noticeable, and nothing seems to get in the way of his nightly wanderings.

Jodl makes his rounds in what civic leaders of El Paso call "the blighted area" — the four or five blocks west of the business district where the cheap Mexican and Chinese cafes, the bus and train depots, the massage parlors and relief missions are located. You can find him there almost every night until twelve — never staying long at any one place and never spending much money; just checking by to have a cup of coffee or pass the time of day with a crony, then moving on.

He usually starts out at the old armed forces YMCA, catching the six o'clock TV news with half a dozen others who are scattered in the rows of straight-backed chairs. He watches until the weather and sports come on, then saunters over to the check-in desk and trades laconic views on world affairs with the balding, cigar-chewing clerk. He doesn't tarry — it's almost as though he were just punching an emotional time clock: "Six twenty-five . . . talking to Benny Weismann." He will slap the desk in a noiseless abrupt parting and go around the corner to the lobby, where he pauses at the magazine rack to thumb through a *Life* or *Post*. After standing a while, scanning an article, he replaces the magazine carefully on the rack and turns around — always on the move again. Shoving his hands into his long tan corduroy jacket and jerking his head briefly toward acquaintances slumped in easy chairs, he continues down the front steps into the street.

After the Y Jodl may go over to Tony's Cafe for coffee and a little early-evening conversation with Candelaria, the fat and pleasant Mexican waitress. He always tries to get in his foreign-language lesson for the day with Candelaria, asking her questions about the meals or the weather in his limited but more or less accurate border Spanish. Tony — standing behind the counter in his dirty white apron and baker's cap — picks his teeth methodically with a toothpick and talks to Jodl without ever really looking at him, staring vacantly across the top of the cash register and out the window. He is a sullen man and speaks in rare and guttural monosyllables, but Jodl likes him. After finishing his coffee and scooting a dime across the counter with his long brown forefinger, Jodl will lean his shoulder past the cash register and pass on to Tony a little piece of confidential something-or-other: a new Nixon joke, a wry comment about city politics or the pleasingly fat waitress. Then shoving both hands back into his coat he goes on out the door. But as he passes along the big front window Jodl usually glances back inside to see if Tony will be chuckling there behind the counter — his hands still clasped almost soldierly behind his back, the toothpick still riding the red moist flesh of his lower lip.

Jodl roams at night partly because he has remained an honest-to-God walker, one of the few men I know who still finds sheer animal pleasure and freedom in moving along on his own two feet. But I think the real reason he stays out on the streets at night is because they are, quite simply, his home. The dank old movie houses, the penny arcade, the dusty news stands, the small hole-in-the-wall liquor stores just big enough for the owners to sit in, entombed among their bottles — they are like a family to him. And when he walks by it's as though he is just casually checking on them, seeing that they are doing all right and are still in place.

Of course he wouldn't admit it — that he has any affection

for train depots or old walk-up hotels. He even denies liking El Paso ("Ahhh, this *town*," he's always telling me; "and these 'senior citizen' types moving west: social security pioneers. . . ." He'll shrug and say, "I think I'll let you have this Golden Age oasis and all these sunning robins. I need San Francisco for a while, something to clot my blood"). And he will take off and I won't see him for a while. But in two or three months he's back. I'll be down on Santa Fe or Durango Street and I'll spot his walk: with his hands shoved deep into his corduroy coat, so that his elbows wing out a little, he will be moving along the sidewalk in his brisk, long-gaited float, never moving so fast he can't reign up in front of a pawn shop to look at the new merchandise or examine a movie advertisement on the side of a building.

Just to look at Jodl, or to meet him briefly, a person would be tempted to think: "Hmmm, a surly, negative fellow — the I've-been-around-and-have-no-more-illusions type." Most of the time he has a somewhat fixed and formal gloominess, his heavy eyebrows pulled together in a slightly doubting frown. And since he is not a smoothly handsome man — with a rather swarthy skin, blemished by pits and perhaps old acne scars — he gives the appearance of a rough-hewn Yugoslavian patriot. His teeth are bad as well, especially toward the back of his mouth, and I think he passes up many a chance to smile because of them.

Yet Jodl, when you know him, is a pleasant and companionable man to be around. I wish I could say he is my friend, but he is such an insistent loner that I doubt he is very close to anyone. Of course he gives the impression of liking it that way — footloose, no strings attached — but I'm not so sure. I wonder if, like the majority of lonely men, he is just somehow unable to tolerate direct emotion. I wonder if it is not as simple as that. For I know that whenever we are talking in a cafe and I happen to say something that amuses him — so that he turns his head slightly in order to look straight at me and make one of his rare, shy forays into smiling — such a loosening of his semi-scowling mask seems to disconcert him. He seems so embarrased at his response — at revealing himself to be so emotionally vulnerable — that he is immediately on edge to leave.

Whenever our chance meetings are over and we give brief nodding farewells outside the cafe, I go on down the street a bit and turn around. I watch as Jodl pauses on the corner, considers, then moves on — as if reassured there were still several hours' worth of cafe-and-window visiting left in him. Always, in that last prolonged look, I have hoped to discover some hidden and significant clue about Jodl. But he has never been interested in providing anyone with clues; he just seems quite content in winging his long-legged, rearing-back way down the street toward nowhere in particular.

IV : *Maids from Juarez*

Ⱳ THE EARLY MORNING *tranvias* come gradually to a stop, the narrow doors fold open, and maids from Juarez spread out along the downtown El Paso streets. At first it is almost as though

whole trainloads of mechanical toys have been bought by some whimsical millionaire and given their freedom. By twos, fours, dozens, the women fan out toward the plaza three blocks away like relentless black-coated and black-scarved dolls. Occasionally they group at street corners — penguins standing at the edge of Antarctic ponds — then, as the light changes, they hurry on.

By nine o'clock the last of them have boarded buses at the plaza and have scattered to their jobs across the city. Had they been dobbed with a bit of radio-reflecting paint as they first emerged from the street cars — and were they then carefully tracked on a radar screen — it would be like tracing the path of arterial blood as it courses from the heart to the farthest capillaries of the body. For no matter where you are during the day — at one of the subdivisions on the north part of town, at the new apartment buildings on the east, near the college on the west — the maids are there: pushing baby carts down sidewalks, sweeping porches, dusting rugs in back yards. They seem virtually omnipresent. You have the feeling that if you got in your car and drove fifty miles straight out into the wildest, most forlorn part of the desert you would find several of them there — one still working, sweeping a salt flat, the other standing patiently in the shade of a scrub mesquite, holding a small paper sack and waiting for the five o'clock Cactus Lines bus. ❧

v : *Negro on the Bench*

W WE HAPPENED TO SIT next to each other in the downtown plaza, this young Negro and I, and began watching a bushy-bearded evangelist try to perform his miracles. The evangelist was standing beside the alligator pond, asking in a loud voice for everyone who had rheumatism, arthritic pains — any kind of illness at all — to come forward and be cured. God could do anything, he said — why not let Him?

It was a sunny noon in March and the park benches were crowded with all the old men in the city who had no better place to go. They sat in their overcoats and hats, some chewing snuff, some hunched forward on their canes, others leaning back and enjoying the peaceful sun.

Judging from the looks of his greasy pants and shoes, I assumed that the young Negro beside me worked in a downtown garage or filling station and, like many others, was just killing time during his lunch hour. He was leaning across his knees, chewing on a match as he watched the evangelist wave his arms and invite those with afflictions to come forward and find their ease.

After a while the evangelist got an old man in a faded blue suit to raise his hand and say that he needed help — he had sinus trouble and asthma. The evangelist put his arm around the old man and asked him to remove his hat while God got ready to perform a miracle.

It went on that way for a while: the evangelist pressing his hands to the old man's head, then jumping back and going off into tongues; the old man standing there with his greasy hat in his hand, looking past the evangelist's beard at his pals and giving a sheepish little grin; the young Negro chewing steadily on his kitchen match and waiting for the miracle.

Yet as I sat there on the bench I found that my mind was not at all on the old man and his sinus trouble; it was on the Negro sitting there at my side — a young man who, though only six inches away, might just as well have been six miles. There was no sense of contact; our races split us apart. I was wondering what to do about it — how to begin the long climb over the walls of alienation and distrust — when my mind said, just talk to him. Just turn toward him a little and say: Look, I don't know you and you don't know me, but there are things we ought to speak about — things that might help to break down the barriers between us. I want to tell you that I am sorry for what my race has done to yours these many past years. I'm sorry that each day, in some fashion or other, you still run the risk of being treated as less than a man. Sure, I know we weren't around when this whole mess started, but we're here now. We've got it on our hands. . . .

That's what my mind wanted. It wanted to do what I had never done before: talk honestly and openly to a Negro. It wanted me not only to start off right but to go ahead and finish, to say: And here's another thing, too. I would like for the day to come when I can sit down here and not even *want* to talk to you — a day when I no longer feel that I should try to help undo the injustices of a half-dozen generations or more. I would like to sit here beside you as any idle person sits beside another on a warm spring day — as two black or two white men would, each paying the other little mind, each simply following the course of his own private thoughts. I really wish things were in that good a shape now, but — well, don't you see? — even if they aren't, a person has to do what he feels he can. . . .

I should have said that and more, but not a word of it came out — and it wasn't because of last-minute moral cowardice or a failure of will. It was just that there are delicacies in relationships that cannot be ignored. No matter who you are and what you feel, you can't go around spilling your insides to a stranger on a park bench at Saturday high noon. That is, you just can't *presume* to. It's not what one human should do to another, Negro or white. So all I did was rise from the park bench after a while and say to the Negro, "Well, I hope you don't have any gall stones that man will want to take out." He laughed, and for a second we looked directly at one another — our eyes meeting in a rather pleasant and, I thought, understanding way.   ⋺

VI : *Bathroom Joys*

AFTER ALL THE ROOMERS HAD GONE to their jobs and she had finished the breakfast dishes in the kitchen, Maria went upstairs and cleaned the big bathroom. She liked it in there with the cool whiteness of the tile floor, the smell of Dreft on the cabinet, the stacks of small white corded towels. She enjoyed the easy way she could move about, setting things down in the quietness and hearing them echo. She liked the little hollow *pock* her broom made whenever she accidentally hit it against the rim of the old tub. And after cleaning the commode she liked to stand beside it and listen to the powerful cleansing sound of the water as it flushed downward, then to the little peaceful singing in the pipes as the bowl refilled.

Sometimes, too, the big lavatory mirror was fun. As she polished it, with the bulb switched on just above, Maria would see her dark hair and slender face and clean starched apron, and she would almost tremble at the beauty of herself in the mirror. She would glance toward the door to see for sure that it was closed, then she would gaze a long while at her stilled image — almost scaring herself with the depth and intimacy of her thrill.

And once, in a very curious way, even the window shade had been exciting. She was pulling down the shade in the window over the tub when it spun away from her and rattled around wildly at the top of the frame before finally coming to rest with a long slow swing of its cord. Maria watched it, delighted, almost tempted to believe the shade was alive. She put her finger back in the ring and this time pulled the shade down more carefully. She adjusted it and turned away to begin her mopping. But somehow she was not satisfied. Leaning her mop against the wall, she went back to the window. She looked at the shade a long moment before pulling the ring down with a jerk — and then giggled as it spun away to the top. She reached up and put her finger in the ring, starting it down again. *Qué bonita*, she said, to the quietness of the big bathroom. And with a smile she began to let the shade go up and down, up and down — entranced by the pleasant, masterful way it pulled against her as if it were a live force, a magnetic energy which uncoiled when she pulled and recoiled when her arm relaxed. ϶

VII : *The Scotsman*

HE WAS A THICK-NECKED, straight-backed slab of a man — a scowling, red-faced Scotsman caught in some kind of deep perplexity. I saw him coming out of the downtown library almost every afternoon — his thick shoulders uncomfortable captives within his tight sweater, his pants legs flapping around his long-striding legs. He had a jutting, Donald Crisp nose that hung belligerently above his sour, down-turned mouth. His jaws were big curved hams. Deep lines slashed between his bushy eyebrows, and his head and bull-like neck rose from his shoulders like a blunted pyramid. His greying hair was always fluffed and ruffled on top, as though he walked against a perpetual wind.

The man seemed wholly out of place there on the sidewalk, frowning at the buildings and passing cars, his face locked in its constant grimace — as though he alone smelled the Secret Pig-pen of the Universe. I thought that, to seem real, the man should have been cresting a hill in some grassy meadow in Aberdeen, with the wind from a nearby loch raising the lapels of his coat and tousling his hair. He ought to have been on his way to beat hell out of a neighbor for going to bed with the man's niece — or perhaps for letting dogs loose on his sheep. In his native sur-roundings he would have had sensible reasons for such immense scowlings — for regarding the very air in front of him with such a blunt intensity.

But outside the El Paso public library he just looked suspicious and childish and lost — as though he had just read that he was made of atoms and would not believe it. Paused on the street corner, staring out at the traffic lights, he seemed to be thinking: "*Atoms* . . . impossible; it's a lie. It's just another goddamn trick to confuse a man." And deep in thought, he would strike out across the street — his hair wild on top, his thick shoulders pulled back, his face set in its angry, puzzled frown.

VIII : *Woman at the Bar*

A SWIMMER, I think to myself: a lean Ohioan who has left her Olympic-sized pool to come sit at the bar in Juarez and drink gin fizzes and try to figure out something about her life. . . . She raises her glass and her blunt fingertips seem rounded by water, the way boulders are; her body is slim, brown, muscular. There is no fat on her; at 27 she is still greyhound lean.

She has the face of a Doge: severe profile, with prominent cheekbones; cheeks sunken just a bit. She would leave a striking death mask. . . .

The young woman drinks at the end of the bar, waiting for her husband to return from a shopping tour. She listens to the long-haired Mexican piano player as he bangs away at request tunes: "Stella by Starlight," "Lover," "Red Roses for a Blue Lady." He has a full, red, satisfied lower lip, and he smiles across at her as he plays. He hits more right notes than wrong ones, and the other women at the bar tap their feet and nod in rhythm.

The vein in the young woman's neck distends, thickens as she talks to the bartender, who is making a frozen daiquiri. She smiles at one of the bartender's comments and instantly her face cracks into planes and angles, into the face of a Zelda Fitzgerald: sharp-edged, silver-painted lips; green, narrow-slitted eyes. Her tanned skin shines warmly in the dim light of the restaurant, and when she crosses her legs in an easy swimmer's motion her sandaled feet angle beautifully.

Her husband returns, carrying packages, and he places them on a stool between them as he sits down. He is a curious physical wreck. His lips and cheeks have fallen, somehow, as if vital facial muscles have been cut. He appears to be unreasonable, suspicious, and almost immediately he begins to sniff the air around the bar — for he *knows* how dropsical his mouth is; he *knows* how tenuously attached his wife is to his money, his social position, his intelligence.

He has a large head, short sandy hair, a thick corpulent neck; he wears amber-rimmed glasses. He stares into his drink and periodically gives long, intense looks down the bar.

Has he intimidated her because of his lawyer prestige and lawyer brains? Does she feel loyalty, pity, secret revulsion? Why did *she* marry *him*: a water nymph joined to a giant, fleshy, tight-mouthed crab? The questions keep shouting themselves. . . .

I finish my drink and begin to steal final glances: Her ear, so intricately convoluted and clean, like a shell washed into the short brown seaweed of her hair; her restless fingers, touching underneath her chin, then sliding absently down the curve of her neck.

Lesbian? Martyr? I cannot figure her out. As the lean, smiling piano player launches into "Rose of Washington Square," I rise to leave — and in passing notice the big vaccination scar on her arm. Almost crimson, it is like a beacon pulsing Save Me, Save Me, in the dim backwaters of the bar. ⮑

IX : *Pan*

ὠ HE REMINDS ME of a neatly kept toothbrush in sun shades.

Each afternoon you will find him sitting alone in the downtown plaza — a spare effiminate man with white hair burred down youthfully to short nylon bristles. Although his thin face is kind of silky and cherubic pink — in keeping with his whole I'm-Really-Quite-A-Young-Man air — he very definitely has false teeth. From time to time he works them about in his mouth with obvious irritation. Usually he wears tight Ivy League pants and black loafers, although occasionally he dresses more casually in starched denims and white sneakers.

It is hard to say how old he is — 45, 60? more, less? For one thing, his white hair is confusing: is it premature, or indicative of advancing years? And his walk: you would think that by looking at the way a man moves you could fairly well estimate his age. But this fellow has neither a middle-aged man's still vigorous tread nor an older one's more halting and labored gait — his effeminacy mixes the labels. Whenever he raises himself from his shady bench he usually does so rather slowly and carefully (— an old man), but then he drifts on down the sidewalk with a rather commendable amount of speed and verve (— middle-aged man or younger.) And woven through both the rising and walking are delicate twists and turnings — the precise mincings and glancing about of a person who wants to see who is watching him and who is not.

Considering him and the paradox of his old man's youthful prance, I sometimes wonder if he doesn't consider himself a useful but neglected Pan. Trim and worldly, his neat cloven hoofs only temporarily stilled within his black loafers, he seems to be waiting for a tribe of followers to gather around him on the grass — to join one another gaily and clap hands before trailing after him from the park to pursue their secret, forbidden delights elsewhere. As he sits there on his bench, alternately frowning at the distasteful presence of his false teeth and lifting his eyebrows at passersby in a kind of guileless, boyish expectancy, he seems on the verge of pulling from the back pocket of his tight black pants a little flute — pulling it out innocently, as if only to practice a while in solitude, but then looking out through the daintily lifted fingers with the steady and uncompromising gaze of a vulture.

x : *Juarez — Summer Days*

W AT FIVE O'CLOCK men just off from work stretch out along the banks of the canal like Steinbeck *paisanos.* They lie sprawled and dirty underneath the cottonwoods, their greasy hats rolled to one side, their legs jackknifed into angles of collapsing rest, their arms flung out on the grass or across their eyes. A few of them lean back on their elbows, chewing grass and looking across the canal into the nearby streets. They talk some, even manage a couple of short-lived lazy laughs, but before long they too succumb to the heat and their tiredness. They roll over — facedown on the grass — and sleep while the crows flap and call above them in the trees.

Across the canal, inside small wooden stands, vendors sell cool drinks from big, open-mouthed jars — beautifully pale lemon- and orange-ade, with chunks of fruit rind floating languidly on top. Customers gathered around the stands drink slowly, taking only small swallows. They seem not to be drinking to quench their thirst as much as to simply be part of a nice social act — to engage in a street corner summer ritual.

Nearby, in the shadows of low adobe buildings, barefooted and long-haired Indian girls from nearby mountains stand in their little islands of solitude, their dark legs powdered almost to the knee with dust from the road and the Juarez streets, their many layers of once-white skirts uniformly darkened — as though they had been carefully washed and re-washed in dirt. The girls press their hands and faces upward toward the passersby, begging in small, faint, fiercely monotoned voices, while behind them old Indian women sit against the buildings and stare into the street — seeing nothing, saying nothing, sunk into the silent caves of their long black shawls.

XI : *Eric the Red*

HE WAS STANDING in the doorway of the hot *tourista* office in Juarez, waiting for the immigration officer to return. He had a small canvas bag, his passport, the clothes on his back — nothing more.

"I-ma-chin my goot luck," he was saying. "In New York I vas reading in de paper vere dey needed somebody who could speak Cherman and do light chobs in dis svank club for shust about sree veeks, and it fit me perfectly, so I got my room and board dere and all se beverages I vanted, and den after dat I vas on my vay again."

He smiled as he talked, seemingly quite at ease about his delay. He stood with his hands clasped behind his back and gazed at a huge map of Mexico on the wall. His long brick-red hair had begun to mat and curl at the nape of his neck, and his nylon shirt carried a stiff body odor. He wore black wool socks and sandals and spoke English carefully, thoughtfully, always hunting for the right word.

"Yes . . . and den from New York to Clearvater, Florida, and Miami Beach. Ho, boy" — he smiled broadly — "dat Miami *Beach!* Sat vas . . . yes, two days ago. And I plan to be back sare in sree veeks — July twenty-one."

He paused and scratched a moment at the scab on his bottom lip. Then he smiled again: "I don't like your U-ni-ted States, I'm afraid. Distances are too . . . yes, too *long.*"

The door in back of us opened and we turned, but it was not the immigration official. A boy sucking a green popsickle padded across in his bare feet, looked out the side window toward a row of parked cars, then padded out again.

"You are American, yes, and do not have to have pictures? Vell "— and he pulled out three small passport photographs from his shirt pocket —" it vas necessary for me to get sese made before lunchtime. Othervise sey do not let me sroo." He shrugged and looked blandly toward the dry riverbed of the Rio Grande. "I vill spend sree days in Chihuahua, no more, and then to Cal-i-for-ni-a, Vancouver, Detroit, Ottova — I vill see some kinfolks dere of my muhser — sen to Boston before Florida once again."

As other tourists began to file into the office — and as the several of us who had been standing for a while grew even more restless and irritable — the young German remained there near the entrance with his cracked, freckled hands behind his back and awaited the pleasure of the casual Mexican official. Immigration, heat, delay — such things were apparently of no consequence to him. With his passport and canvas bag, and the three required photographs, he was in excellent shape. And besides, wasn't he going to be in Miami Beach on July twenty-one?

We fidgeted, paced, sighed. The young German fingered his scab and smiled into the map of Mexico.

Texas Journal

I : *Counter Girl*

⚜ YOU WATCH HER WHITE HANDS reach into the soapy water — hands with blue veins pleasantly distended; hands not muscular, yet knowledgeable of work.

Her arms are bare, and alabaster white. The dim veins are like blue shadows in vases of milk.

She holds a pair of dripping glasses for a moment, waves them gently, sets them to one side. The water gleams on her hands and arms. When she bends again to the sink, her full breasts push against the front of her white apron.

"Coffee, sir? Black, or with cream. . . .?" She has turned to the counter now, smiling and drying her hands a little with her apron. She faces you as though you were her first customer of the day. She has a pleasant lilt to her voice, a readiness to please. She does not seem to mind that it is five o'clock in the afternoon on a hot, July day.

Who is this young woman, you wonder, and what is she doing here in the drugstore? You watch her careful, graceful movements. . . . Yes, she knows about work; she is not frustrated and embittered among the ham sandwiches and dirty coffee cups. And as she took your order she had looked at you directly — her eyes seeming watchful and knowing.

The young woman sets the coffee quietly before you, smiling a brief smile; then she turns back to the sink. Her hands are immersed once more in the soapy water and her breasts press against the apron. Her dark hair falls forward a little, baring her neck. She continues to work dutifully as the ceiling fan whirs and the glasses drain on the damp side board. ⟳

II : *Fields, Mountains, Clouds*

⚜ I SAT LOOKING into the cotton fields—into masses of greenery that were astonishing in richness, magnificent in depth. Row after row, silent and growing in the steady summer heat, they made an endless plenitude of leaves. Mere plants, yes — routinely hoed and watered and fertilized — but God Almighty, how much more than that. . . . What could beauty be if not such acres as those — leaves whitely radiant with sun on their tops, superbly shadowed beneath.

And rising above such voluptuous seas: the mountains. While the fields below stretched forth in a multitudinous green — touched by the sun in a hundred pleasing ways — the mountains loomed serenely, offering grandeur to the sky. Strong, smoky-blue, their outline etched cleanly by distance, they grew out of the desert like a range of gods.

And in the sky itself — on that day of stunning, absolute, almost holy blue — clouds went about their business in private and imperious ways. They were like celestial magicians in strange white boats, drifting in from the horizon to perform their subtleties above the earth. To smudge, expand, congregate, burst; to burn with white fire or dissolve into space — it was all the same to these elegant tricksters of the air.

. . . For a while, sitting in the shade of a cottonwood, I watched, hypnotized, as one huge, dazzling cloud unwound itself in the midday light. At first it seemed content just to lazily explode — to boil luxuriously within its own wild cataracts — but finally it started on its long upward climb. And though it was doomed to achieve no real end — to do no more than lunge upward and then splash vaguely, ineptly, to one side — it had, for a moment, the genuine thrust of life. Probing into the fiercely illuminated sky, the cloud was like some strange formless beast that was seeking a freer, a more beautiful, a more gigantic self in the limitless ocean of air.

III : *Robin Hood*

W I WAS SEATED IN THE CAR at a shopping center, reading *The Catcher in the Rye* on a rather cheerless winter day, when a woman walked past—an average-faced, ordinary-figured woman of thirty-three or so. And as I looked at her I suddenly thought: I like humans; I like them better than I would gods. The thought pleased me, so I watched the woman more closely as she went along the sidewalk. Even though she was carrying a big sack of groceries and was facing into the wind, she nipped on by with a rather pleasant expression on her face — not letting things get at her too much, apparently; taking the day and grocery shopping and all the little inglorious human routines pretty well in stride. . . .

Then I noticed that she had on a bit of foolishness — an extravagantly jaunty pair of soft-leather, slip-on "archer's shoes": the Robin Hood kind. The shoes pleased me immensely, for it occurred to me that with her little air of *accepting* things, and with those shoes, she would certainly manage to get by: she would bear her children and endure the long stretches of monotony in her days and occassionally she might even catch out of the sudden stillness of an afternoon some scrap of the mystery and poetry in life — or perhaps just the plain incomprehensibility of things. Thus she would manage to touch most of the bases as she went — blindfolded, like the rest of us — around the infield of God's strange Polo Grounds.

And because this nice-walking, pleasing human-friend was so totally ordinary, so wholly un-outstanding — and so touched by folly with her Sherwood Forest slippers — I felt a surge of delight and I began musing in Salinger's Old Sally way: Old human . . . old fallible, unspectacular, enduring human . . . old blindly continuing, carrying-things-off-pretty-well human being.

As the woman slowly disappeared down the street with her groceries, I wanted to jump out of the car and run over to her and pin a small medal on her silly archer's shoes. I wanted to let her know she had been watched and judged and found Good. For it did not matter to me whether or not she carried out her destiny with any special honor or dignity; she at least functioned in the world with a touch of grace. That alone, I felt, was enough to merit attention and honor on a dull November day. ⟿

IV : *Solitary Women*

W AFTER SIX IN THE EVENING they occupy the side booths of Shilo's Delicatessen in San Antonio, slowly giving way to loneliness under the guiding hand of recorded violin music and Michelob beer. They sit with their hats on, in neat brown suits, now and then turning their heads to stare across to adjoining tables. Sometimes I have caught them staring straight at me, unabashed, as if staring were a bitter right they had earned over the years.

To these women the booths at Shilo's are secure caves they can crawl into with dignity at the end of the day. They don't have to hope there; they do not have to feel too hopelessly lost or lonely. They can simply wait for a while, suspended and watchful, like pendulums after the springs run down. ⟿

V : *Tom*

W WHENEVER I WATERED THE LAWN in the late afternoon I would look across the driveway into our neighbor's yard: Tom, our cat, would usually be sitting there under a big elm tree, having a bowel movement. Always supremely composed, he pretended not to see me. He must have sat on that stretch of shadowed dirt and Bermuda grass a dozen times a day, and each time you would have thought he was waiting for a parade to pass by, or the arrival of the Three Wise Men, or else was simply doing God's work. But that was his way; Tom had a great sense of style.

He's dead now — buried under a castor bean bush in a Fort Worth back yard — and I miss him. He understood about a lot of things, and was a great pal.

We went on walks together late at night. Tom would by lying on the front porch bannister — sleeping or resting or waiting, whatever it is that cats do when they are still and on porches — and at the first sound of the screen door opening Tom would spring down from the bannister and lope off across the lawn. It had somehow become a gentleman's agreement that he was to take one side of the street and I the other, and on those terms the two of us would strike out underneath the midnight trees. Since we moved casually along, never hurrying, never headed any place in particular, Tom indulged whatever fancies he had about sniffing lantana bushes or half-buried candy wrappers or the sides of houses. He would stay at a place in order to smell it — lagging far behind — then with long bounding arcs he would streak down the sidewalk to catch up.

Tom didn't mind where we went as long as we stayed within the familiar, friendly darkness and the heavily shadowed trees. But he could never adjust to the alien territory of the Toddle House. It was down the street six or seven blocks at the corner of a thoroughfare, and he would wait outside, obviously ill at ease, while I stopped in there occasionally for coffee. The flashing neon signs reflecting on the sidewalk, the high blue arc lights making their strange daylight along the thoroughfare, the stark brightness of the Toddle House itself just beyond the big plate glass — they all put Tom on guard, made him fearful and primitive. He stayed by the wire newspaper rack until I came outside again, then shot ahead toward the dark streets of home.

Tom had a variety of interests and was a shade more speculative, I think, than most cats. He was fascinated by all narrow openings and would stand in front of a vent or shaft for long stretches of time. He became interested in our neighbors' unused fireplace and whenever he could slip into their house he would go into their dark living room to stare at it. I saw him there a number of times — peering up into its luring darkness like a contemplative Frenchman gazing at the frame of an unfinished skyscraper. I could almost see the pipe stuck within his whiskers, and the soft gray cap.

He was poisoned one hot Fourth of July — two weeks before we were to leave Fort Worth. I found him lunging drunkenly through a flower bed early in the morning, but I thought he had just eaten a little spoiled food the night before. The veterinarians I called were not working that day so I took him to the shade of the garage, laid him on a towsack, and put out some water. His insides were heaving and he was groaning deep in his body.

By three in the afternoon he was dead. I found him stretched out under the bedroom window cooler, with flies gathering at his nose. I didn't know what else to do so I carried him into the shadows of the garden and dug a hole and laid him in.

I kept feeling, afterwards, that I had badly neglected him — that I had carelessly let him die. And for a long time whenever I came across pictures of him in my daughter's scrapbook — the same old Tom, alive, charming and blasé as hell — I would wish, again, that it had not been the Fourth of July, that the vets had not been off fishing, that I had tried a more drastic kind of first aid.

I guess what finally laid his ghost for me was when my daughter asked if cats had a heaven. I said I didn't see why not, and then I began to think about it — about Tom up there in a cat paradise. I could see him staring unperturbably into some intriguing celestial crevice and then, nonchalantly, relieving himself on a passing cloud. With great prowlings through the eternal night, and sniffing among galaxies — why, it all fit, of course. Heaven was right up Tom's alley. ⋧

VI : *Grona's Lumber Yard*

❦ MR. GRONA IS CLOSING OUT. At 81 he is ready to work more in his garden and sit more on his small wooden porch that faces the Junction highway. He has had a For Sale sign in his office display window for over a year now, but no one seems interested in buying a lumber yard in a small hill country town.

I was back in his store recently, buying some paint and turpentine and screen wire. Mr. Grona looked the same as always, wearing his faded khakis and straw hat, but he seemed a little more willing to smile and take his time than he used to be — maybe because at 81 he is ready to admit that getting a pound's worth of nails weighed or a two-by-four sawed isn't quite as important to him as it once was.

He has been letting his stock run down — not reordering — so he had to look around a bit before locating the gallon of gray enamel that I wanted. When he found it he blew the dust off the lid and then took the can outside to the paint shaker that was mounted on the wall beside the lumber bins. I followed him, and it was there, under a big oak tree, while the gallon of enamel vibrated and Mr. Grona waited patiently in his old straw hat, that I thought about Mr. Grona's grandson and how pleasant it would be for a boy to be helping out in a place like the lumber yard.

The grandson had been there in the office, sitting next to the window fan, when I came in — a blue eyed, snub-nosed boy in a white T-shirt. He helped hold down one end of a roll of screen wire while Mr. Grona measured it; he chewed gum and listened while Mr. Grona told me about trying to sell the store; he ran to a storage room and brought back the can of turpentine I needed. He stood behind the counter and doodled with a pencil; once he answered the phone.

As I stood in the shade, with a two o'clock breeze coasting up the open space of the gravel yard, I thought not only of Mr. Grona's grandson but also of how Sherwood Anderson worked in a bicycle shop when he was growing up in Ohio. That had always seemed rather nice to me — a kid working among the smells of lubricating oils and new tires and leather seats. It was human-sized labor that was direct and personal. You could learn how to be an apprentice in a trade but you could also eavesdrop comfortably on the day-to-day routines of the adult world you would be entering soon.

I stared out into the heat and wished that my son — when he became eleven or so — would be able to spend a summer helping out in a casually run lumber yard. I wished he could fall into the rhythms and routines of waiting on customers — finding out their habits and peculiarities — as well as learning about bolts and paints and window moldings and cement. I wished he could get the feel of such a place and value it and have it make good memories for him. . . .

The paint vibrator stopped and Mr. Grona took the can out of the clamps and held it close to his ear and shook it. He smiled as the enamel in the can made a loose sloshing sound that showed it was well mixed.

We went back inside the office and Mr. Grona itemized on a pad what I had bought — with his grandson looking over his elbow. Then I paid him, gathered up my supplies, and went out to the trunk of my car.

The For Sale sign behind the display glass — faded from the many afternoons of sun — wasn't very eye-catching. I doubted that anyone would be interested in buying the lumber yard: Mr. Grona would probably just lock the doors one day and let them stay locked while he sat on his front porch across the highway.

I closed the trunk and got into my car, wondering if there would be a lumber yard — or feed store, or corner grocery store — that my son could work in some day, in some small town. I wondered if he could run back to a storeroom to find a can of turpentine for a customer, or if such businesses in such small towns would soon be as much of the past as Sherwood Anderson's bicycle shop.

VII : *They Should Have Been There*

THEY OUGHT to have been there.

They ought to have been walking down the streets of Juarez and come within a block of their parked cars — ready to return across the bridge to middle-class America — and they ought to have looked down at the sidewalk. They ought to have stopped, as I did, in the head-pounding July sun and seen the mother begin to unwrap the bundle of rags she was holding as she sat there beside a building, moaning. That was what it looked like, at least — just a bundle of gray woolens picked up from a *ropa usada* store.

And then as the woman in her old scarf and faded skirt and gray wool coat gradually pulled aside the rags of her bundle, they ought to have been looking down over my shoulder. They would not have minded the heat any longer, or for that matter remembered where they were going, or what country they were in, or whose politics they preferred: they would not have even cared to remember what their names were.

Because all they could have thought about was this human *something* that the woman had just laid bare. . . . A child? Surely not; their minds would not have accepted that. Surely that wizened little creature with its gnome-like head — that skull of stretched skin and scattered hair: surely one could not possibly call that a *girl*, or a *baby*. . . . And that little vine of a body: surely that length of grotesquely shrunken chest and legs was a skinned rabbit or squirrel. That could not be a — what had someone once called it: a fleshly temple of the immortal soul?

Yes, indeed, they should have been there. Because if they had, they might have accomplished much more than I. For at first all I did was stand there and stare. Then, finally, I turned to a man sitting nearby on a curb and asked in my poor Spanish, Is it dead? The man shrugged and said he didn't think so. When two shoe shine boys came up I put out my hand and asked them: Is it dead? . . . I kept thinking that the woman, in her grief, was simply carrying the child around, wrapping and unwrapping it with her rags, refusing to admit that the baby had died.

But no, the boys said, it was alive. It was two months old and needed milk and medicines, and the woman had no money. She had other children at home, but she was too poor to buy things for any of them.

Well, what would others have done? They would have perhaps taken charge in a more effective way, would have managed things better: indeed, would have so completely discharged their moral responsibilities to that woman and her dying little girl that later, whenever they took a bite of food or relaxed in a movie or smiled at a clever joke they would not automatically have that child appear before their eyes — lying there on the sidewalk looking a hundred years old and with its mouth finally beginning to work in a soundless cry; with its mother, bent over, moaning, wiping its excrement away with its own covering rags.

Me? I just did things in the usual American way: I took out my wallet and gave the boys some money. . . . Sure, I was upset, concerned, and I explained to the boys that the mother must go to a doctor and that she must do exactly what he said. And after the boys gave the money to the woman she slowly gathered up the child and the three of them started off toward a doctor's office two blocks away. I stood there on the street corner and watched until she went through the doctor's door.

I got into my car and drove on across the bridge, thinking about my own child. She was four years old — firm-legged, cheerful, healthy. She was taking ballet once a week at the YWCA, and sometimes at night she would fly around the living room in little sweeping ballet prancings. She was beautifully alive and vibrant.

When I got home I looked at her and could not help feeling guilty as the guiltiest dog. For not three miles away still another ruined little fragment of a human being (one of how many: a dozen? a hundred? a thousand?) was probably lying in its bundle of rough rags.

What I wanted to know was: Who was to blame? Did you blame Mexico as a country; God as a Creator; Juarez as a poverty-filled town? The man sitting on the curb? the shoe shine boys? the father? The mother: should you blame her for being poor and perhaps ignorant and out of work? Or the child: maybe blame it for not being born stronger? Or blame me, for not staying there and doing more? . . . *Nobody?* . . . Don't blame anyone — just say, Well, that's life?

. . . They just should have been there, that's all — those who always have an answer for the world's problems. Then maybe I could have learned how you deal with poverty. ⇝

Portraits in Nostalgia: A Diary

IT WAS A STRANGE and rather poignant world I lived in once — that small junior high school set among the palms of its small, easy-going seacoast town. For nine months of a year I, as teacher, knew the rhythm of that world, felt its every change. Then it vanished, and I was left wondering what it meant: all those faces, all those lives. . . .

SEPTEMBER 20. Julio has started coming in before class each morning to read. A good-looking Mexican-American boy—athletic, very imaginative, very self-conscious about his race—he will not study but he loves to read. So I have begun feeding him books. He finds a new one on his desk twice a week — some of my own, some from the town library, whatever I think he can grasp. I have seen him in the room many mornings when I come up the walk. He doesn't hunch over his desk but sits up straight, appearing quite proud, as though the room were his own private sanctuary. I never speak to him about the books, since they represent an undeclared pact. He never mentions them either except occasionally. Sometimes at the beginning of class he will twist up to my desk in his shy, athletic way and say, "Boy, that Don Camillo. You know . . . well, he sure was some guy, don't you think? It's a shame you can't actually meet people like that — a guy that really knows what to do."

OCTOBER 19. At fourteen Clifford looks out warily from behind thick glasses and plays his trombone with a remarkable and precocious skill. Small, sensitive, and very bright, he suffers his adolescence strongly and is rarely able to escape its burden. He has a soulmate in Freddie Burns and together they manage to carry their daily crosses. Only music takes the weight from Clifford's soul and makes him free.

This afternoon I went up to the second floor and watched the band go through its football drill. The Gulf breeze had died down and left a sticky calm; the practice field was dusty. The band members, worn out from marching up and down the chalk lines, let their march tune get thinner and thinner until it was just a wail of trumpets and weak rattle of drums. Everyone was dispirited; everything seemed to be dragging at the heels.

Then they stopped to make the formation for the school football queen, and I saw Clifford step out to the microphone at the edge of the field to play his trombone solo. He walked with his stabbing, dogged, self-conscious steps — his sweaty, black-rimmed glasses slipped down on his nose, his shoes and blue jeans dusty, his red sport shirt circled dark with sweat underneath his arms. Yet despite the heat and the dust, despite the music that began blowing loose from the lyres on the band members' horns — despite the frail cries of the clarinets and dull, off-tone monotonies from the French horns — Clifford grimly sought his muse. He stood there on the little wooden platform, angled his slide upward toward a thin line of clouds over the coast, and played "I'm Getting Sentimental Over You" while chill bumps spread over my arms and up my back. It was as though he had a bag of glory in his horn and was emptying it all right there on the fifty-yard line. ⮑

NOVEMBER 23. Ah, pleasant Helen, shyly but eagerly laughing Helen, rustling into class with her many petticoats and starched dress, scented not with fragrant powders but with clean, blooming youth, well-brushed hair, toothpaste, home, excitement, innocence: Helen of the House of Kaufmann, the polite, quiet, yet vigorous Teuton of the farmlands of South Texas, vibrant and eager after her early morning bus ride from the country. She sits on the front row in class, her lessons neatly prepared, her pen filled, her pencil sharpened, her eyes ready to learn. She sits there each day, not boldly but ready, her head lowered just slightly in shyness but her gaze direct. She is radiant with health and well-scrubbed life.

And music. But it is resting quietly inside her now; she is not too full of melancholy yet because there are still so many things to take the edge off: basketball, homework, the girls' trio, and sometimes boys. But the music will be coming along, steadily, and the quietness will begin to grow larger. Music is the big thing in her life, though she doesn't know it yet. ⇝

DECEMBER 5. Sitting upright at his desk, with his mouth half open, his light-blond eyelashes arched, and a "It wasn't me — honest!" expression, Andy Holmes looks each day like a friendly polar bear waiting to be tossed a mullet. And that's what makes it so sad, in a way — that constant look of innocence and in-comprehension. For you know he will go through life itself a little wide-eyed and open-mouthed, a little surprised at things going badly, never quite comprehending, always just a shade too slow.

But he gets to drive a jeep to school and sit in it at noon with his friends under the shade of the palm trees, and that's what counts most with Andy. And since his mother is pretty and his father a lawyer who wears a jaunty golf cap and gets a long new car each year, he will continue to stay popular and will con-tinue to get by. He will just have to go through life half-turned around, that's all: not indignant, merely surprised at the turn of events. Even on the football field the play generally goes one way and Andy another.

JANUARY 18. We're working on a play in the afternoons. For a week and a half now the cast has met after school in the hollow, musty auditorium for "Destiny Rides the Rails." It is a fine melo-drama, loaded with perilous situations and heavily drawn char-acters. Sam Harvey is the villain and he smirks and stalks about the stage, twirling his imaginary moustaches, hissing asides to

{ 141 }

the audience, rolling his eyes almost out of socket with pretended shocks and surprises; and Suzanne, the heroine, flings herself over the cardboard railroad tracks again and again with beautiful abandon.

While they wait for their cues some of the cast sit on the back steps behind the auditorium, watching lazy games of tennis across the way, smelling incinerator smoke — absorbing the atmosphere that remains about the grounds when the classrooms are finally empty for the day. And though they laugh and talk and drink innumerable cokes they never quite shove out of their consciousness this one new and important fact that has suddenly elevated them: that they are actors, grouped and dedicated to a common cause; that together they have entered the temple of art, and have been heightened. ⟩

FEBRUARY 3. After school Cora Lopez works in Barton's Drug Store, picking up paper cups and straws and glasses. A tall, slim Mexican-American girl who wears bright orange lipstick and orange sweaters, she will probably go to school one more year at the most and then marry or work full time at the drug store. She doesn't like or dislike school; it doesn't impinge enough on her to force any particular feeling. School is simply better than home, where all the little sisters are, and she can meet her boy friends there and play baseball with them at noon or talk under the palms by the coast road. She doesn't particularly like or dislike working in the drug store, either, but since she has to work to help support her family, it is as good a job for her as any. And she seems to fit there. She moves languidly about the booths and tables, spreading a little absent-minded charm among the high school boys who saunter in after school to drink cokes and read funny books and scratch. ⟩

FEBRUARY 19. More than anything else, Edna Nabors wants to be popular. Each afternoon as she waits for the school bus, she hopes that a sudden wave of popularity will come storming around the corner of the grounds instead of the old yellow bus and that it will sweep her up in a glittering cloud above the school and will make people stop and say, "Why, look — it's Edna Nabors!" Sometimes she would settle for just being able to walk down town with some of the other eighth grade girls in their confident groups of four and five — laughing, giggling, watching over their shoulder for boys. But nothing ever happens. She just goes on standing in line: taller, bigger, and carrying more books than the other children who live on her route. She waits, knowing her chances for winning happiness are melting away, and she thinks, Maybe tomorrow . . . maybe if I do my hair different, like Glenda. . . . Maybe. . . . But the bus rounds the corner and the sixth and seventh graders grab up their books and lunch pails, and Edna is forced to move slowly along with them, headed for another long bouncing ride into the country and another uneventful day's end. ➤

MARCH 5. My day would not be complete without little Paul and his sense of humor. Each morning he waits for me at the front steps with some kind of tale. It may be about a visitor's encounter in the living room with Sam, his mountain boomer lizard, or perhaps about the neighbor girl who got her pigtail caught in the roller of an old-fashioned washing machine. Maybe it will be about how the principal walked in as Mrs. Wittik, the fat social studies teacher, was trying to secretly adjust her brassiere strap in front of the office mirror. It is usually a small event, but Paul knows how to find the essential flavor of a thing. At 14 he has discovered human frailty. ➤

APRIL 17. Suzanne: Already solitary and prim, as finely sculptured as a cool thin vase or some isolated water bird seen at a distance in an ankle-deep bay. Temperamental, loyal, and long-suffering, with great doe eyes and fragile hands, she feels she has the artist's flair but knows that it only makes her unhappy and lonely and a little unpopular. She comes to the Wednesday night creative writing club in the library and sits very poised and erect while she writes gravely in her beautiful slanting hand about Love in Old Monterrey.　　　　　　　　　　　　　 ⋺

MAY 4. Maybelle plays the flute in the junior high band, and almost every lunch hour she returns to her home room to prac-tice — patiently covering the rings in her flute with her white pudgy fingers, consistently patting her foot out of time. She is industrious in all things, turning the simplest of home work as-signments into elaborate projects for research. She loves to use the family encyclopedia at night and copies from it for hours — wanting very much to please, hoping that the many carefully copied sheets, held together so neatly by three paper clips, will bring surprised and appreciative comments on her scholarliness.

Maybelle lives to work and to please. At the Teen Club dances in the elementary cafeteria she is always the first to arrive, carry-ing armloads of paper cups and cookies and prizes. And during the party she bustles around with a motherly seeing-eye, tacking up crepe paper streamers that have drooped from the wall, ladling out punch, getting new ping pong balls from the closet to replace the crushed ones. By the end of the party she is glow-ing with the tiredness of joyful service, and her smile is almost beatific. Her upper lip has a little moustache of sweat, and to her it is as worthy as any jeweled crown.

Jolly, companionable, hardworking Maybelle — never the queen of the ball but always its enduring and loving hand-maiden.　　　　　　　　　　　　　　　　　　　　　 ⋺

A Saturday Visitor

W IT WAS SATURDAY MORNING in Austin and the day of the big football game. We had got up late at the boarding house, my brother and his two college roommates and I, and had gone around the corner to a drugstore for cups of coffee. We sat for a while — the three of them talking and smoking and drinking coffee while I sipped at a glass of water — then we started off on a casual tour of the campus area that lasted until dinnertime.

Although I was just ten or eleven at the time, it was as though I had already read *Ulysses* and could thus recognize in my brother and his two friends a little troupe of sober, serious Buck Mulligans, leisurely strolling about the Dublinesque streets and talking to one another in their incomprehensible jargon. At first I tried listening to the strange, interminable words: "bourgeoisie . . . Dostoevski . . . Dos Passos." But I soon gave up, accepting the sound of them as a kind of verbal ferris wheel that was to turn continually above my head.

I remember that once during the morning I spoke tentatively of breakfast, but there was no reaction so afterward I remained quiet. We continued to drift on down the many tree-lined campus streets, in and out of boarding houses and conversations with tousle-haired young men still bedded in dark rooms. I soon lost any desire to enjoy this, my first trip around a college; I was getting too tired and too hungry. I was no longer even concerned about walking — about where and when to direct my steps. I simply wanted to remain true to my one last conscious need: to follow the long crack between my brother's right arm and his body and finally end up at a place where I could sit down.

As the quarter and half hours passed by, the reality of the morning gradually smudged and faded. My brother and his friends, and even the streets and the buildings, began to take on a kind of depthless, cardboard quality, like scenery in a play. It was as though we had walked so much and so far that we had finally walked straight out of reality and into a dream.

(I remember standing once on the corner of a busy intersection at the bottom of a hill. As I waited, the street before me ceased to be an ordinary street of concrete and stoplights and curbs, and became, somehow, a stretch of light gray water. Cars were racing past each other out in midstream like boats in a weird regatta, all with flags and streamers and the arms of white-shirted young men hanging in the windows. And as I glanced up at the three companions of my dream who were standing beside me — looking tranquilly out across the water — they appeared perfectly at home, as though it were simply their habit to stroll together each morning as we had done and ultimately wind up there to muse a while beside the small inland bay).

It was sometime after twelve when we entered our last boarding house. At the sound of the opening front door heads of young men slid out from behind the pages of newspapers like those of mechanical dummies. They were out at all angles, watching us file across the living room toward the kitchen. As we passed they receded one by one behind the pages — like puppet heads drawn slowly off stage.

In the kitchen a small woman with white hair and a flowered apron patted me on the shoulder while my brother spoke some words to her about breakfast. She seated me at a long table with a clean tablecloth, and after a while the Negro cook brought me sausage and eggs. I remember how strange the food on the plate looked at dinnertime — as if it were not food at all but miniature lifeless figures stretched out on a round china slab: the three dark-brown Brookfield sausages resembling shriveled, bald-headed slaves and the two white-frilled fried eggs their heat-prostrated mistresses. I looked at the plate a long time, and the more I looked the more I began to remember how desperately

I had wanted breakfast all morning long – until finally I was so overwhelmed by hunger that I could not eat.

I asked the cook where the bathroom was, and she very kindly pointed the way down the hall. But when I reached it I was out of luck there too: it was not just an ordinary bathroom, like the kind I used back home, but a holy temple of cleanliness, with sweet-smelling soaps and deodorizers and powders spread a-round like incense. It seemed out of the question to violate the sanctity of the commode, so I closed the door quietly and left without doing my business. I went back to the living room. The young men were standing around in twos and threes, or sitting in front of windows, looking out, or lounging on the sofa behind the walls of their newspapers. Almost all were holding coffee cups now, some loudly discussing the afternoon game, some talking in the manner of my brother and his two friends – oblivious to everything except the steady sounds of their serious mouths.

For a while I sat and watched the shoe polish can on the fire-place mantel, and ties hanging on the backs of chairs. I smelled the bitterness of the sofa – a smell like a number of old un-washed dogs. The gas burning in the wall grates clung heavily and oppressively to the air, as though trying to wear it down and finally displace it so that no one could breathe. Newspapers turned incessantly in the room, their steady crackling like the popping of distant siege guns. And outside there were heavy cars that kept lunging uphill toward the football stadium.

It was here, in this heightened, close, unreal place, that I be-gan trying to remember something that seemed important: who, or what, had I been all those many mornings before I started out on this one? What had happened to that person I had always known so familiarly as Me? Almost frantically I worked for an answer – right up to the moment when my head grew lighter and things began to swim in the room and I passed out cold under the whatnot stand. ⟐

Suzy

W SUZY WASN'T BEAUTIFUL — not the way boys think college girls ought to be beautiful. She wore her hair cut short and brushed to the back of her neck in a kind of ducktail, she was skinnyish and she had freckles scattered across her forehead and underneath her eyes. But somehow you never got around to thinking about classic features when you looked at Suzy; you never remembered to see anything except her fluid grace, or cloudy blue eyes, or that childlike, almost beatific smile that curved up just enough — a smile as fresh and pure as morning.

I met her one afternoon at a park near the campus, on a day that was falling all over itself with spring. Children were yelling "Annie-Over" far across the baseball field, the trees were bursting with lushness — almost screaming inside themselves, "We're green! We're green!" — and black grackles were everywhere, wheezing and gliding through the clean dampness coming up from the creek.

I was lying on the grass, trying to study, when I glanced up and saw her standing on the narrow wooden bridge that arched across the creek. She was looking at me — her arms folded over her breast, holding her books — and she was smiling. Maybe it was that smile, or the way her head was tilted back, with a long pencil angled through her hair, or the shine of her pink sweater in the sunlight; maybe it was just me, feeling lonesome. Maybe it was the deep-green afternoon. Whatever it was, it was enough to make me brush the grass off my pants and walk over to her.

We talked for a little while casually, and then, holding her books with one arm, she carefully began to pick grass off my shirt. Maybe that was part of it too — her touching me so easily and naturally, almost intimately, as if she were reaching over and straightening her husband's collar at a train-station farewell. I asked her if she wanted to swing on the swings, the afternoon being so pleasant and all. She laughed and nodded yes, and together we strolled off across the shadowed, four-o'clock grass.

That's how it was in the beginning — the two of us just walking along through those great, dimmed spaces of cathedral light, saying half-cautious, half-excited words. We let our hands trail idly against the trees in passing, and when we got to the swings Suzy put her books on the ground with a pleasing and exact efficiency — as though she had long before rehearsed and mastered the minor physical business of how to place books — and then she sat on one of the boards and I began to push her. She made a lovely sight: her slim legs pointed toward the surrounding trees, her head dropped back into a kind of wild-Indian pose, her laugh drifting behind her like a banner in the lazy air of the park.

There was no real sequence to the days that followed. Time became a kaleidoscopic present, with days and places revolving around us like fragments of pastel-colored glass. We took prodigious walks, roaming across town in the long, spacious afternoons. We found snake-spit cones glistening like snow in the weeds of the vacant lots, and tire swings filled with birds' nests in people's yards. We watched small boys sitting alone in wagons, crying, while their older sisters left them on the sidewalk and ran inside the house and never came out; and in a downtown alley a small, amber Pekingese stared down at us from a dirty second-story window with sad, squinting eyes. And once we found a fat green caterpillar with orange stripes curled on the glossy leaf of a magnolia tree. We put him in an empty jar and carried him with us — lying on his piece of leaf like a small, indolent Buddha.

Sometimes we went to a vacant lot behind Suzy's dormitory, where brush and boards were piled high in the tall grass. I would first poke around to see about snakes and then both of us would crawl deep into the grass. The afternoon sunlight just barely filtered through, and the heavy, rotting smells of lumber and grass sent up a heady incense. We would sit there side by side, doing some of our best talking — about jazz, and Thurber, and how good the smell of shrimp was on your hands when you went fishing down on the Gulf coast.

And I think it was there, in that snug brush cave, that Suzy told me about the time she broke her arm — how she had dressed up in a black robe and floppy hat and jumped out her window one night into a fraternity pinning party on the lawn, yelling that she was Cyrano de Bergerac falling from the moon. I can still hear that laugh of hers when she was tickled by her own tales. It always seemed to touch her inside and excite something deep and sensitive and almost sexual. She would laugh and tighten her body and bring her elbows in close to her sides, as if wanting to keep the laughter within her as long as possible and enjoy its exquisite richness.

Love? Well, yes, but not at first — not when we were just barreling along across the days. I don't think I loved anything in the beginning except my own sense of freedom, my own joy. We were too delighted in the sense and touch of each other, too pleased with ourselves and the days.

Then one afternoon something happened — not much, really, just an inevitable refocusing on familiar things. We met as usual after our last class, went walking, and on our way back to the campus stopped at a drugstore. It was a hot day and the ceiling fan was going lazily around, blowing a little Dr. Pepper sign at the end of a string. We were just sitting there in a booth, spooning away at our ice cream, when we happened to glance over at the sign and then back at each other. I don't know what it was, exactly, but at that moment we seemed to *perceive* each other — to understand in a split second how strange and awesome another person actually is.

I remember that we glanced back down and began eating

again in our first self-conscious silence. We knew a curious thing had happened — as though we had accidentally seen each other naked — so we toyed with our paper napkins and pretended to watch people passing by on the sidewalk. We kept sneaking glances across the table and always caught the other watching. Even after we left the drugstore the new awkwardness persisted, and as we walked back to Suzy's dormitory we spoke to each other with shy, almost courteous words.

It was later the same week, I think, the night we went to hear Louis Armstrong at a dance over on the east side of town, that I first realized what Suzy meant to me. It was during intermission, when I left our table and went to find the men's room. I had put my hand on the rest-room door and turned around to look back at Suzy — and just seeing her made my heart jump. I guess it was her being there alone, in the middle of all the cigarette haze and white tablecloths and surging bodies. She was holding her glass in that special way of hers — not casually or idly, but almost earnestly, clasping it tightly the way a child would. Perhaps it was simply that — her looking so isolated, so incomplete without me there beside her; or maybe it was her sitting so erect and motionless, as if suddenly fixed in time and space. I don't know what I saw or what it meant, but right then I felt the first strange stir of love.

Afterward we walked down the moonlit streets. We swung our hands and sang loud bars of foolish songs while dogs ran out to the fences and barked. I remember that I could just barely make out the figures of people sitting on their dark front porches, talking about us in low voices. And I remember too that we finally stopped somewhere in a vacant lot beneath a lone, shadowing tree, and while cars with bouncing headlights rattled by and the lush spring night throbbed around us, we held each other as if the only reality in the world were made of lips and hands and warm, moist skin.

It was about the middle of May, with the final exams right on us, that we decided to study out at the lake on the edge of town. I was going to borrow my cousin's car so we could start out early and make a day of it. But when I got to her dormitory the house-mother told me Suzy was feeling sick and probably didn't want to go out. Suzy was in the kitchen, she said, if I wanted to talk to her.

I found her perched on a little kitchen serving table, peeling an orange. She had on blue jeans and a man's long-sleeved shirt with the tail hanging out. Her face was pale and the freckles on her forehead stood out like little scabs. She looked worn and thin and pitiful and ugly. At first she started to smile — to make some kind of joke of it all — then suddenly she jumped off the table and ran to the sink and vomited. I held her, bracing her shoulders and putting my hand across her forehead, and after a while she shuddered and sank against me. I got a dish towel and wiped her face. (Looking back on it now, it seems almost like a kind of primitive marriage ceremony: holding her tightly, vowing with-out words to protect her, in sickness and in health.)

Suzy went to bed after that, but when I went back in the after-noon she was feeling better. She got her books and we drove out toward the lake. It was a fine, warm afternoon, and as we drove past the new subdivision houses their crushed-tile roofs were blazing in the sun. We turned onto a partly graded road and stopped in front of a long ravine that ran down to the edge of the lake. There were a lot of Spanish oaks and sycamores rimming the ravine, and when I turned off the motor we sat for a long while listening to the leaves moving in the breeze coming off the water. Suzy wanted the sound up close, so I got out and cut some branches from the trees and then stuck them around the car. For the rest of the afternoon we listened to leaves scraping lazily across the windshield while we studied.

When it was dusk we walked down into the ravine. The air was heavy and chilled, and birds on the hillsides made frantic little settling noises for a while; then, as if finally smothered by the dampness and gathering silence, they were still. There was an immense quiet, and as we walked across the floor of the ravine the twigs broke beneath our feet with intimate, brittle sounds.

After it became fully dark we sat on the ground against a log, Suzy's arms around my legs and her head in my lap. I ran my hand slowly over her face and lips and across her hair, and I began to tell her how it would be when we were married. I don't remember all the words, but I told her how we would get a cabin on some mountainside out West, and how we would go down every morning to the lake below and watch some old fisherman give us his toothless, bless-you-young-folks smile. I told her how we would speak to everybody along the bank and examine all the early catches, and how every now and then we would look at each other and want to touch so badly we couldn't stand it. I told her how in the afternoons, about dark, we would go outside our cabin and put our arms around each other and watch the lights blinking on down below.

And I was just getting started, actually — telling how later on we would have children, a couple of really terrific kids — when I felt the wetness of her face on my arm and her moving away from me, saying, "Oh, honey, stop, please stop, I can't stand it any more," and heard her crying hard against the ground.

I did not know, of course, that for four years she had been engaged — that in June she was to be married to a West Point cadet beneath crossed swords. She had never mentioned this home-town boy friend of hers, and I had never bothered to ask if there was anyone else. Maybe she had kept stalling for time, hoping to find an easy way to tell me — or perhaps, as her roommate insisted later, she was actually going to break off the engagement. I can't say. All I know is that that afternoon at the lake was our last day together. Before the week was out she flew to New York, leaving her books and a closet half full of clothes. She didn't take her exams or even say good-by.

I have never quite figured out that long, intimate spring; it has remained an unfinished chapter in my life. And although I gradually came to accept the end of it, and Suzy, I am even now, ten years later, strongly susceptible to memories of her. Whenever I walk down some fresh-smelling, tree-lined street I can almost hear, once again, Joe Mooney singing "Nina Never Knew" on a car radio and feel Suzy's slim, taut body swinging along close to mine. I can still visualize the way her hair strung down across her cheeks as she waited for me on a street corner in a pouring rain — can almost see her fingertips as she took my face in her hands because it was April and life was good and we were in love. ⦚

Zzzz The Clown

W SOMETIMES when I would hear music that made chill bumps climb my backbone and my heart grow large a little and then melt, I would end up thinking about young doctor Adam Whitehouse, that lonely man back in Texas who had such feelings too. I would recall the times late at night in his bachelor's quarters at the V.A. hospital, when we sat listening to Wagner or Beethoven or the old sentimental cowboy songs he loved so well — when the only realities for us were the soaring sound of the music, the single lampshade throwing its soft red glow about the room, and the bottle of Jack Daniels whiskey sitting between us on the floor.

And if I got to thinking hard about those times, about the music and the quiet sharing of thoughts, I would find myself with a sudden case of Adam Whitehouse nostalgia. I would have a sudden desire to materialize him before me in a typical pose — to greet him again, say, at a moment when he was already committed to flight, at a moment when he stood beside his car at the hospital BOQ some late afternoon after work, dressed not as you would expect a doctor to be dressed but in khakis and a black Stetson hat, his hand reaching for the car door and a cigarette already in his mouth (yet not just a cigarette, not just something casually and momentarily appended to his mouth, but something which at that particular time of day was as vital to him as his car and his hat and the road into the country — something warm and undemanding and friendly, something safe and perhaps even comforting: his car cigarette, his travelling-companion cigarette). I wanted to materialize him strongly enough that I could see that very cigarette up to his mouth and his hard, almost tortoise-shell fingernail already engaged in snapping a kitchen match into flame with a single mechanical thrust.

Yet as Adam stood there — in my vision — under the heavy afternoon shadow of the sidewalk oaks, I knew he would not

want to see me. He would not want to see anyone. All he wished was to be able to open his car door and escape into the country and solitude. And even though he had been suddenly trapped by the demands of my visit it would only be for a moment. He did not have the slightest intention of allowing me or any other person alive to lure him away just then from the cave of his privacy into the bright glare of human concourse.

So I understood: he would remain only briefly on the side-walk curb, erect and motionless, quietly waiting the conversation out. He would be gracious yet reserved and wary, his face turned away just slightly so that I would end up talking to his profile and to the quick dartings of his almost Indian-black eyes. Now and then he would rock his head and black hat and shoulders slightly forward in stiff nods of agreement or understanding — complete and unequivocal perceptions of what I had in mind, the kind of nods that God would give, perhaps, if a creator from another world dropped by for a visit and began chattering away about an excellent new method he had hit on for starting something he called Life.

Yet regardless of how compelling such nostalgia was to start with, no matter how genuinely glad I was to revisit Adam, inevitably my thoughts of him would go sour and my mind would begin to retreat from the memory of his constant elusiveness and eccentricities: "But damn it all," I would say, blurting into the hollow heart of my disappearing mood, "why can't he be like other people? Why is he always running away, always ducking out?" And with the screw of frustration and anger turning a little tighter, I would go on to a harsher blaze of words: "My God, who do these 'superior' guys like Adam think they are? What leads them to believe they can treat people any way they want to and still end up with friends? . . . But that's just it, of course; these superior ones, these ultra-talented, they don't need any friends. That's their big secret and their strength. They don't need anyone but themselves. They've got everything they want right inside them, right in the middle of those big blossomed egos."

After a main course of this kind of grumbling and growling I would end up sampling little bitter, random thoughts for dessert — about the "cult of the superman" and the "rights of genius." I formed my words strongly; I would have fists doubled up all over me. And in a final offensive move to demonstrate the truth and righteousness of my position, I would quickly begin to tally up a dozen or more people who, in shining contrast to Adam, had never been "difficult," had always been considerate, out-going, easy to be around; had always been. . . . But it would be no use. By then the wind would have blown out of me. And though I still resisted using it I knew the word I would have finally had to use — to describe the considerate, easy-going ones — would be dull. Extremely dull. Most of all, dull.

After the hard burst of anger was over and I was rid of my spleen, I would be left free to indulge again — this time even more widely, and objectively, than before — in thoughts about Adam, back when he had just started working at the veterans' hospital in a little town in central Texas and the two of us had occasionally shared conversation and long nights of music. And I was free, too, to realize that in my anger I had been like a small boy who is frustrated because there can't be his favorite kind of party all the time, with his favorite kind of people — who keeps jumping up and down and asking, Well why isn't Adam going to come? Why won't he leave his hiding place and tell us some more stories? Why doesn't he just act nice and come over and play like everybody else?

It was difficult for me to accept that there were people in the world who existed in a special class by themselves — who, like the sun or an ocean constituted a kind of special phenomenon and had to be accepted on their own terms or not at all. Adam, as just this kind of phenomenon, was hard for me, and everyone else, to deal with and comprehend. Much of the time he was simply exasperating. I suppose he stood head and shoulders above all the phenomenal exasperators I ever knew, and it was impossible during any given year's time not to have the urge to shout at him in a kind of violent, final despair: All right, have it your own way, Adam. Just keep on burrowing your private escape-hole deeper into the earth — or else hide there in your room in the BOQ and padlock it and then sink the whole thing in a vat of cement. For no one is going to give a damn. No one is going to waste any more energy trying to get you to respond to the normal social urges — or keep coming around to seek you out. No one is going to violate that precious, holy privacy of yours any more. Just go right ahead — rot in triumphant secrecy. No one cares.

But of course those of us who liked Adam did care, couldn't help but care — couldn't help but keep wishing that someday he would finally break down and join the human race. We felt that he had talents and brain power to equip half a dozen lesser men; we also felt that despite his good work at the hospital, and despite all his skillfully executed hobbies, he was not really using those brains and talents — at least, not using them constructively, publicly, in a way that would cause him to rise above his fellow men to the eminence he deserved. And all of us, too, had the same set of questions to keep rising in our minds: Was Adam really content to live such a private kind of life? At 37, and going along as he was, would he ever marry? Was he laboring, perhaps, under some secret yearning, or some secret sorrow? Was Adam Whitehouse someone for people to envy, or to pity, or someone to be finally shrugged off and let alone? But no one's curiosity was ever really satisfied. Adam kept right on going his puzzling, solitary way — kept right on tending to his many known pursuits and perhaps an equal number of unknown ones. He remained squarely where he had always been — behind his mask: the capable doctor, the excellent occasional companion, the young man of brilliant potentials, the constant enigma.

I knew that Adam was extremely uncomfortable around people — was perhaps frightened of the sheer press and number of them, of their constant demands — yet I also knew that during working hours at the hospital he was seemingly at ease. It was as if when he worked there among all the wasting old tuberculars and cancer patients, trying to lessen some of their pains, he could always manage to keep them at the right emotional distance. His low precise soothing voice, his starched white jacket, his professional air — they composed a wall around him that no patient could ever climb. He could be quite comfortable and secure. It was only when five o'clock rolled around and his life became his own again — when the door of his office was finally closed and he had made the last rounds on his ward and had returned to his bachelor quarters' room: it was only then that the wall disappeared. He was alone, without a diagnosis to make, an x-ray to read, a medical competence to indulge in. It was during these long, weighted hours until nine o'clock the next morning — hours when he was stripped of his title and his public function and was simply Adam Whitehouse, exposed, vulnerable human being — that he was forced to build an even higher and stronger wall, one made from the most familiar and trustworthy materials he knew: his own genius and solitude.

And Adam was so cock-eyed talented, so nearly self-sufficient, that he could almost pull off the business of living within that wall in a world of himself. I had been around him enough to know that he could lead an astonishingly-sustained private life — and creative one. On the afternoons when he didn't drive out into the country he would come home to that big, double room of his and not leave it again until time for work the next morning.

He would spend hours building hi-fi sets or drawing house plans or making pieces of furniture. Sometimes he would paint pictures of horses in oils — good pictures that he would hang up for a week or so and then destroy. Food he never seemed to care about. He ate with no particular system or enjoyment: at night a meal might be a couple of cigarettes or a can of bean dip, or perhaps Fritos and beer. Many times he would not eat at all and instead would practice on his flute. Sometimes, too, if the mood was right, he took out of his closet an ancient fiddle that his grandfather had once used and he would play for a long while — until he began to think of what Heifetz sounded like, how Heifetz would make the same notes, and then he would put the fiddle back in the closet behind the pillow cases full of empty beer cans and the dirty laundry. Or perhaps he would stay up most of the night reading or writing or listening to music.

On those rare occasions when he had done all that he could possibly do by himself — and had convinced himself that he could tolerate the close association of people — he would invite someone over to that spartan yet chaotic room of his. Sometimes I would come alone, sometimes there would be other casual and close friends. If he had been drinking a lot — as usually he had been, in order to prepare himself for the meetings — he would occasionally be quite voluable and would tell anecdotes about his nights as an intern in New Orleans, or perhaps long, involved sagas of his kinfolks in East Texas and their bitter feuds. Sometimes he described in great detail the peculiar habits of skunks or armadillos that he had observed during his boyhood days on a ranch. Most of the time, however, he would just sit in a chair holding his glass of Jack Daniels — listening, nodding, sometimes chuckling soundlessly over someone's penetrating remark. His body and shoulders would jerk a little when he laughed this way, and it always seemed that he was not laughing at what you thought he was but instead was exercising a kind of oblique, private mirth — a bemused amusement that Lewis Carroll might have understood and shared. Yet to me it was this very laughter, this quick, nodding affirmative response, that made Adam appear saddest and most alone; for even though he moved his shoulders in real-enough good humor it seemed that if he shook them just a little harder and a little longer he would go beyond laughing and end up shaking with tears.

It was on just such a night that I listened to a story of his about Zzzz the clown. It was past midnight and only the two of us were there in his room. We had been listening to music for a long while when, in the middle of a Beethoven symphony, Adam put his whiskey glass on the floor near his chair and rose in that formal, arrow-straight way of his—precisely like an Indian brave rising from a campfire to perform some kind of blood ritual — and strode into the adjoining darkened room. From a tall stack of hi-fi manuals and sketch pads and pocket books he drew out several pages of typewritten paper and came back to his chair. He picked up his drink and under the soft glow of the red table lamp he began to read — in the way which no other human reads, in a clipped, cadenced, hesitant, sometimes almost wrathful softness. The manuscript had no title but it told of Zzzz, a country boy who needed friendship and understanding and love, and who finally became a clown:

Zzzz — so the story went — grew up on a ranch in the hill country of Texas. He was a shy boy who liked to read and make crystal radio sets and ride horseback around the ranch. His father was a half-Cherokee who raised sheep and goats enough to make a living but who never really cared to do anything much except stand in some off-place by the barn and stare out into the hills and valleys. The boy's mother died when Zzzz was four — died of what, the boy could never quite say. All he could remember was a dark room and his mother's hair falling loose about her pillow and his father standing by himself on the small back porch. Below the ranchhouse was a clear river with high white bluffs, and Zzzz used to take his favorite books there to read — *How Green Was My Valley, The Red Pony, The Yearling*. He would sit for hours in one of the small caliche caves in the bluffs, reading and then gazing out across the river. The characters in the books were like a family to him, and their sorrows became his: Gabilan was his own red pony that wandered out in the brush to die, Fodderwing his own crippled pal in the Florida everglades.

Adam never looked up at me as he read, never tried to gauge my reaction. When he finished his drink he poured himself another one without breaking the flow of words or even taking his eyes from the page:

But — he continued — there came a time when Zzzz could no longer sit his silent hours in the caves along the river. He had gone his final day to the country schoolhouse, had amazed his teachers for the last time with his feats of learning, and was leaving the familiar cedar hills and agarita bushes to become a doctor. Zzzz was now a silent, formal young man who had taken to wearing a round-topped gunfighter's black hat; who had been judged by the outside world and found to be brilliant. . . .

"Brilliant" — what a mocking, wrathful, taunting ring Adam gave to the word as he read it. He hung it on the air like a venomous thing righteously exposed, and then sat there for a moment afterwards, rocking his head and shoulders a little, his mouth pulled slightly open as though it were full of the bitter aftertaste of the word.

Adam read on, telling how Zzzz indeed became a doctor but also a clown, a strange and elusive performer hiding behind his mask. He told how Zzzz worked year after year behind the mask, adding little touches of paint to it as any good clown should — deepening the red nose of drunken public buffoonery, adding new layers of deathly-white to the cheeks of tragic sorrow, widening the mouth with enigmatic stripes and shadows, circling the eyes to set off their piercing brilliance. Zzzz was never quite sure, though, if the mask was what people had finally decided that they wanted to see, or if it was what he himself actually wanted to wear. But since it worked so successfully, fooling most of all those who thought they knew him best, Zzzz became afraid to pull it off, afraid to show himself as he really was. So he went his solitary way, ostensibly aloof and self-possessed, daring only in moments of drunkenness — when the whiskey that he had poured into himself to keep the mask in place had ironically washed it away — daring only then to approach a person he valued and ask tentatively, shyly, almost apologetically: "Would you...do...me...the honor of...allowing me to...call you... my friend?"

I had not been looking at Adam while he read. Soon after he began his story I had turned my head slightly, focusing toward the floor in order to concentrate better on the sound of his voice and the words. But when I heard the question of Zzzz's, so carefully and haltingly spoken, I knew from the shift in tone that Adam had stopped reading downward into the manuscript and was saying those words in my direction. I glanced up, just quickly enough to catch him looking at me. He did not acknowledge the glance, however, and immediately rose from his chair — a bit unsteady but nevertheless straight-backed and wholly in command of himself. He said that we had perhaps heard enough of Zzzz for one night, that it was late, that unless he got some sleep he would never make it to work on time the next morning. He was so distant and formal, so completely withdrawn into himself again, that for a moment I was almost willing to gamble everything — the whole relationship, such as it was — and say, All right, now, Adam: stop. Don't usher me out. This time we're going to stick right here and say whatever needs to be said and it is not going to be about any X-Y-Z somebody but about you. We're going to leave off the masks and just sit here bare-faced and vulnerable. Hell, man, finding a friend is not hard if you want to be one yourself. . . .

But I couldn't do it; I couldn't bulldoze someone like Adam into confidences or lecture him with platitudes. It would have violated his sense of dignity and my own as well. So I bade him goodnight, reluctantly, and left, knowing that I would never hear any more about Zzzz the clown — that he would return to the stack of hi-fi manuals and sketch pads, alone and intact. I knew also that Adam would not go to bed at all that night. Instead he would pour himself another drink, the biggest of the entire evening, and after putting on another Beethoven record he would sit in his chair under the small red glow of light until morning, dozing some, sipping Jack Daniels some, but mostly thinking — God knows what.   ⋙

ACKNOWLEDGEMENTS

Some of these sketches and stories appeared originally in *The Texas Observer, Southwest Review, Redbook, New Mexico Quarterly, Descant, Latitudes,* and *Southwesterner,* and they are reprinted with permission.